Rogues

LIDDY MIDNIGHT
CRICKET STARR

ELLORA'S CAVE
ROMANTICA PUBLISHING

What the critics are saying...

&

"An exhilarating story that is sure to heat up many cold winter nights." ~ *Coffee Time Romance*

"Rogues is a great book that is fun to read with a great plot. This is not just a vampire or a shifter book. It is not just a ménage book, nor is it just a mystery. The combination of the three create a fun, entertaining, and sexy book that is hard to put down and will keep you enthralled throughout the entire story." ~ *TwoLips Reviews*

"An exciting, wonderful read. It is full of laughs and actions. Liddy Midnight and Cricket Starr created a story with a wonderful plot and a group of people you cannot help but love. Rogues was an absolute joy to read from start to finish." ~ *Fallen Angels Reviews*

"There is nothing quite like a book that starts out with a hot sex scene in the very first sentence. Rogues makes promises with that first line, and mostly delivers on them." ~ *Gottawritenetwork*

"An intergalactic frolic full of thrills, chills and sex so hot it will steam up your screen makes Rogues a definite keeper." ~ *Erotic-escapades*

"ROGUES is a thrilling novel of intrigue, hot sex, lots of laughter, and unforgettable characters." ~ *Romantic Junkies*

An Ellora's Cave Romantica Publication

www.ellorascave.com

Rogues

ISBN 9781419953330
ALL RIGHTS RESERVED.
Rogues Copyright © 2006 Liddy Midnight & Cricket Starr
Edited by Raelene Gorlinsky
Cover art by Syneca

This Book Printed in the U.S.A. by Jasmine-Jade Enterprises, LLC.

Electronic book Publication August 2006
Trade paperback Publication June 2007

Excerpt from *I'll Be Hunting You* Copyright © Shiloh Walker, 2007

Content Advisory:

S – ENSUOUS
E – ROTIC
X – TREME

Ellora's Cave Publishing offers three levels of Romantica® reading entertainment: S (S-ensuous), E (E-rotic), and X (X-treme).

The following material contains graphic sexual content meant for mature readers. This story has been rated E–rotic.

S-*ensuous* love scenes are explicit and leave nothing to the imagination.

E-*rotic* love scenes are explicit, leave nothing to the imagination, and are high in volume per the overall word count. E-rated titles might contain material that some readers find objectionable—in other words, almost anything goes, sexually. E-rated titles are the most graphic titles we carry in terms of both sexual language and descriptiveness in these works of literature.

X-*treme* titles differ from E-rated titles only in plot premise and storyline execution. Stories designated with the letter X tend to contain difficult or controversial subject matter not for the faint of heart.

Also by Cricket Starr

&

Divine Interventions 1: Violet among the Roses
Divine Interventions 2: Echo in the Hall
Divine Interventions 3: Nemesis of the Garden
Ellora's Cavemen: Dreams of the Oasis lll *(anthology)*
Ellora's Cavemen: Legendary Tails I *(anthology)*
Ghosts of Christmas Past
Holiday Reflections *(anthology)*
Hollywood after Dark: Fangs for the Memories
Memories Revised
Memories to Come
Perfect Hero
The Doll
Two Men and a Lady *(anthology)*

If you are a fan of Cricket's Hollywood After Dark vampire stories, be sure to see the first in the series, All Night Inn, at Cerridwen Press (www.cerridwenpress.com), written under the name Janet Miller.

About the Authors

෨

Liddy Midnight lives, loves, works and writes in the woods of eastern Pennsylvania, surrounded by lush greenery and wildlife. Although raccoons, possums, skunks and the occasional fox eat the cat food on her back porch, she's no more than half an hour from some of the finest shopping in the country. Situated in this best of all possible worlds, how could she write anything other than romance?

Cricket Starr lives in the San Francisco Bay area with her husband of more years than she chooses to count. She loves fantasies, particularly sexual fantasies, and sees her writing as an opportunity to test boundaries. Her driving ambition is to have more fun than anyone should or could have. While published in other venues under her own name, she's found a home for her erotica writing here at Ellora's Cave.

Liddy and Cricket welcome comments from readers. You can find their websites and email addresses on their author bio pages at www.ellorascave.com.

Tell Us What You Think

We appreciate hearing reader opinions about our books. You can email us at Comments@EllorasCave.com.

ROGUES

∽

Dedication

&

To Raelene, who has the best fantasies. She knows what she wants, knows how to ask for it, and may be careful about doing either in the future.

Chapter One

∞

"A vampire, a psychic and a werewolf walk into a bar on Alpha Prime…" — *1001 Stellar Jokes*

"Don't you ever wish we had a woman around?" Thomas asked from his position on the bunk. Impressive in his nudity, the dark-haired vampire lounged against the ship's cabin wall, one hand idly stroking his massive erection.

Rick paused in applying oil to his own cock long enough to give his lover a speculative look. Had he thought of a woman? Sometimes…not just any woman, but one woman in particular. Had Thomas felt her mental presence too? No, he'd referred to a generic woman.

Now that was hardly flattering. Rick pinned his partner with a long-suffering glare. "Why do you always pick the worst times to bring up things like this? And don't argue. You know you do."

Thomas laughed, letting his close-set fangs show. The distance between them was exactly that of the twin scars on Rick's neck, marks that designated him a vampire companion. For thirty years Rick had carried those scars and been Thomas' principal blood donor — decades of exploring space and aging very little.

The two men had chosen each other well. Rick's psychic skills and practicality made him a perfect companion for Thomas, and Rick could never be comfortable in a relationship where he didn't pull his own weight. The pair often shared minds. Being compatible — a necessity on long interstellar trips cooped up in what amounted to little more than a large metal box—and ambivalently oriented sexually, they'd become lovers as well as partners in their mostly legit trading activities.

Their current cargo was very legit, consisting of staples and medical supplies for a new colony and luxury goods for several planets on the way back. No rush, no worries about inspections or questionable documents, just a routine run during which they could relax and enjoy themselves.

In anticipation of their coming fuck, Rick opened himself up mentally. The familiar warm glow of Thomas' mind brushed his.

"I was just thinking. It would be nice to have someone else around." When Rick's head jerked up and he drew back, Thomas added quickly, "It's not that I wish you were a woman."

"Thank the stars for that." Rick carried the oil to the bed and pushed Thomas to lie on his stomach. One hand began to spread the oil over his anus, carefully massaging it in. "I'd hate to think you were going straight on me."

Thomas surrendered himself to the pleasure of the moment. Oh gods, Rick had good hands. Gentle when they should be, strong when needed. With a little heartfelt moan of pleasure, he relaxed against the mattress, lifting his ass in invitation. "No chance of that, I still like men...or at least I like you that way. I can't imagine not having you around. But sometimes I miss having a woman. They're soft, sweet." Rick's finger, slick with oil, probed his ass and he groaned at the welcome invasion. "Gentle." A second finger entered him and he gasped in pleasure. "And they like to cuddle."

"Maybe we should just get a dog." Rick snorted and pulled his hand away.

Thomas' anus felt cold and empty. The sensation just amplified his desire for a woman. They could share, both be alpha instead of taking turns. What a rush that would be!

Linking minds while they both pumped their way to a mind-blowing orgasm. Shared, of course. Idly, he wondered if a three-way mind link was possible. And if so, what it would feel like.

"Don't be an ass. You can't fuck a dog, and you know that's what I want. Someone with breasts and more than one hole. I want someone with a pussy." He glanced slyly over his shoulder. "So do you. I can see your thoughts when we're joined."

Suiting action to his words, he let his opened mind make contact with the glowing haze of Rick's essence. Sweet Sol, even with a partial link, he could feel Rick's hands on him, at the same time feeling the tight muscles of his ass relax under Rick's firm massage. He pulled back, waiting for Rick to complete the link.

Rick knelt on the bed between Thomas' legs, spreading them with his knees. He leaned over his partner's back, placing himself right up against Thomas' puckered ass, but he hesitated over his friend's words.

Of course it was true…he did sometimes fantasize about women. Well, not women in general—one woman in particular. Someone special.

He'd never met her and had no idea who she was, but there was someone he felt sometimes when he and Thomas were together like this, their minds joined. He had no image of her, didn't know what she looked like, but he sensed her mind…or more the lack of her presence. He felt a noticeable void, one that should be filled. Thomas hadn't said anything before, but apparently he too felt the woman's absence and knew she was part of them that was missing.

It was one of the reasons Rick loved making love, for those moments when he could sense the shadow of her as part of their joining, as if he could see into the future. He wasn't prescient, at least that had never been part of his talent, but at times he sensed her.

She was out there, somewhere, waiting for them to find her. A woman made for the two of them—the woman who would make them all complete.

A shudder that was only partially desire slid through him. The golden glow of Thomas' mind hovered just outside of his as a purple lust-ridden haze descended across his own thoughts. That's how he saw their minds when they were linked, gold and purple, but there was something off-kilter. Something should be there that wasn't. Some other color.

He let his cock tease his lover's puckered opening for a moment before easing the tip just inside the tight ring of flesh. Every time they made love, he was grateful that fate had brought him into Thomas' life and bed.

No longer worried about their missing third, he dimly heard Thomas moan something unintelligible into the pillow. Closing his eyes, Rick opened up his mind to Thomas' golden glow and let them melt together.

"Could we talk about this later?" Rick asked, just before plunging deep inside his vampire lover.

Thomas gave a long, sensuous moan. "Oh, I suppose," he gasped.

Three hard thrusts later neither of them was thinking about anything but how good it felt. For Rick, Thomas' ass was tight and welcoming and the only place he wanted to be at the moment.

He reached around to find his partner's cock, rock-hard and weeping for attention. Rick started a slow pump along the shaft, his hand still well-oiled. Sexual tension changed Thomas' glow from bright sunshine to a deep gold.

Yes, like that…so good. Thomas' mental voice was a near prayer. *Just like that. You always know what I need.*

After all these years, I should, was Rick's tart answer. Whether he was using his psi powers or not, he did know what it took to give Thomas pleasure.

He slid his other arm onto the bed near Thomas' head, inches from his mouth and sharp fangs. *I know everything you need.* Even as ancient as Thomas was, he still needed blood when he made love. Rick was happy to supply whatever his partner required. With their minds linked, he shared all of Thomas' emotions. The ecstasy of feeding while climaxing was beyond anything a norm could imagine.

The vampire drew his proffered wrist closer and gave it a slow lick that sent waves of pleasure coursing through Rick. As if teasing him, Thomas did it again and again, until Rick couldn't bear the suspense any longer.

Bite me, you fool! He stroked out, until just the head of his cock rested inside the tight circle of muscle.

Thomas' response was a mental chuckle before his fangs dug deep into Rick's wrist, the flash of pain momentary and a mere enhancement. Involuntarily, Rick bucked hard against his lover's ass, his cock driving deeper and harder than before.

Both men moaned, mentally and aloud. Their minds flowed together. Rick tasted his own blood on Thomas' tongue while Thomas knew how tight his ass felt around Rick's cock. Filling and being filled.

Thomas sucked hard and swallowed, the heady essence of his lover nearly bringing him to orgasm. Rick's hand sped up on his cock to hasten it along. As sex clouded the vampire's mind, Rick felt something else rise, a bloodlust dark and powerful.

Left unchecked, a vampire engaged in sex could be dangerous, drinking until his lover died. Even through the haze of purple-gold sensual delight, Rick had to maintain some control over Thomas' feeding or risk losing his life. His death would most likely mean Thomas' as well. Few vampires got over the shock of killing a companion that way, most choosing suicide shortly after.

This was when Rick most missed the woman he thought of as their third, when he couldn't completely abandon himself. He sometimes thought that, if he had another to help maintain the link, they could all three indulge in the ultimate pleasure without risking any of their lives.

For a moment he let himself go and reveled in the feel of Thomas under him, feeding from him, tight around him and firm in his hand. It was so good.

So very good.

The combined haze of their link seduced him further and he let his control slip.

So very, very good.

Just on the edge of his consciousness Rick saw a hint of color—a halo of bright light like a sunrise on the horizon, but when he turned his attention to it, the dawn colors disappeared in a burst of green.

Enough! It was as if the flash of color had somehow broken Thomas' bloodlust. On his own, he pulled back and licked Rick's wrist, erasing the wounds as if they'd never been. Rick had barely gotten over his surprise at that when Thomas' cock began to pulse wildly, erupting in his hand.

The vampire's orgasm fed his own and Rick exploded as Thomas' ass milked his come from him.

Afterward both men lay collapsed on the bed, arms and legs entangled, minds joined but gradually separating until they were each themselves again. The smell of sex and blood permeated the air of the cabin, mixed with the headiness of masculine sweat. Rick breathed deeply of it, enjoying it, letting satisfaction wash over him. He'd actually lost control for a moment and it had been glorious.

Thomas recovered first, pushing himself up to stare at his companion. "What the fuck was that?"

"Huh?" Rick startled out of his relaxed daze. "What do you mean?"

"You lost control. I was feeding and you stopped controlling the link." The vampire was breathing hard, panic sharpening his voice. "In a heartbeat, everything went dark. All I could taste was you and I just couldn't get enough. I wasn't going to stop. *I wasn't going to stop,*" Thomas repeated, his eyes wide with horror. "You know what that would have meant. Then there was this green light and it broke through the bloodlust." His eyes narrowed as Rick suppressed a smile. "You know what that was, don't you?"

"I don't, not really. It's just a feeling I've gotten a couple of times," Rick said. "Like something's coming…or someone." He tilted his head back against the wall and gazed at the metal ceiling as if he could see through it into the future. The smile broke through. "Something good, I think."

"Something female?" Thomas' voice lost its edge and he grinned in anticipation, eyes glowing the way they did when intense emotions gripped him.

"Possibly. And this was the strongest I've ever felt it." Rick laughed and pushed his hair out of his eyes. Thomas never could hold a grudge, especially when a promise was dangled in front of him. "We're due in at Sedilous tomorrow. Let's see what shows up."

* * * * *

Sedilous was one of the original space outposts set up after the first galactic war as a way station between star systems. The entire place was amazing both in how decrepit it was and how functional it remained despite its condition. Activity hummed around it. Shuttles ran back and forth between the station and their mother ships, while the smaller vessels packed the yard.

For a moment, Rick was transported back to his childhood, watching a swarm of bees in a field. He slammed the door shut on that memory, shoving it back where it belonged, far in the past.

They tucked the *Sleepwalker* into a slot between a luxury yacht and a packet—far enough from the station entry to ensure privacy but not far enough to hamper a hasty departure.

Rick ducked under a string of half-burned-out party lights, into the darkness of the bar. As his eyes adjusted to the low light, he surveyed the crowd.

A motley group of spacers, similar to those who had been here the last time they docked, lounged around the bar. A hatchet-faced old man wearing a tattered Imperial jacket raised a hand in greeting. Rick looked closer and revised his opinion. Nope, not similar—most of them *were* the same spacers who'd been here before.

"Hard times?" he whispered to Thomas. "Old Morgan looks like he hasn't moved since we left last year."

"Maybe he hasn't. Word on Jiggy was that his wife finally died."

One of the better-dressed men in the place sidled up to them. His suit was fairly new and his hair had been cut recently. "Hey, guys, got any news worth paying for? I'll arrange for a top-dollar consideration." A few other men with the same appearance, as though they had all been stamped out in the same factory, waited a discreet distance away.

Rick grinned. "Well, if it isn't our old pal George! Who are you working for now?"

George's carefully schooled features broke into a satisfied smile. "I went independent two months ago, became an info-factor. I can arrange sales to a variety of buyers. Got anything worthwhile?" George signaled for a round of drinks. "My sponsors pay my expenses. Not a bad deal."

"You've come up in the world. Congratulations!" Thomas clapped George on the shoulder. "Sorry, we've been on a long run. Haven't heard anything useful for six months. What's hot these days?"

The barkeep set the glasses up on the bar. George led the way and passed them around. Lowering his voice and leaning closer, he cast a glance at the other suits before he spoke. "I've got one client interested in anything involving sterile manufacturing advances and another looking for a source of high-quality emeralds." He ticked the items off on his fingers. "Someone's flooding the black market with lab animals—good pedigrees, standard DNA lines—and I know who wants to know who it is and where they're getting them. Then, there's the age-old question of the meaning of life."

"Everyone wants to know that one. Too bad, we can't help you today." Thomas was already looking out over the room, gaze lingering on anyone remotely female in appearance. Leave it to the vampire to lose interest so quickly when there was the prospect of pussy.

"How about transporting a cargo? No questions asked, excellent pay."

Rick focused on George. Possibly an opportunity, if the destination coincided with their run to Deltan. They had plenty of room left for more goods. They'd often carried cargoes for more than one destination—and more than one shipper, unbeknownst to the others—in the past. A sweet deal all around, double pay for the same run. "How big a load and where to?"

George's gaze sharpened. He lowered his voice again. "The *Sleepwalker* can handle it, no sweat. The destination's a rendezvous on a research station out beyond Cumin."

A day and a half round-trip, max. Rick sighed. That was tempting, very tempting. "Not too far, but it's the wrong direction. We've got a load of med supplies on contract and we can't afford any delays."

George straightened. His expression became bland once more. "Maybe next time."

Mindful that they might find George useful in the future, Rick shook his hand. "Thanks for the drinks."

"Let me know if you come up with anything I can use. I'm always here." George handed out his card with a tight smile and faded into the background.

A discordant tune started up, blasting through the ceiling speakers. Zydeco-opera fusion. Rick hadn't heard that in almost a decade. He'd hoped never to encounter it again and certainly not at that volume. Thomas flinched, muttering a curse, and Rick was glad for once they weren't mentally linked. The noise grated enough on his normal ears. He didn't want to know what it sounded like to his hypersensitive partner.

The scattered tables held some couples but mostly same-sex crews enjoying their chosen poison. He nodded to a few he knew and eyed those he didn't recognize. This early, he wasn't about to try to be heard over the music and the other patrons shouting at each other. No sense in getting hoarse as well as deaf right off the bat.

You never knew who you'd find here, from bounty hunters looking to make a collar to spies for every corporation and government agency imaginable. Since the Empire fell apart, knowledge was the edge everyone wanted.

Thomas glanced around at the women with eager eyes. "So do you see her yet?" His words were audible over the hubbub of drunks and partiers. Although he'd clearly meant to whisper, he might as well have used an amplifier.

Use our link, dammit. Rick couldn't restrain himself from shushing his partner.

Thomas tossed off a nevertheless sincere, *Sorry.* He turned his attention back to the women in the bar. *There's one who might do, no, she looks too rough.*

His partner's contrition lasted for one word, no more. As usual, Thomas didn't mean to blab their business to the whole crowd. He was just enthusiastic. Rick sighed. Knowledge was power and in places like this, power was a valuable commodity. Time after time, he'd tried to instill a bit of discretion in his partner. To no avail.

Thomas was at least a hundred years older than he was...so why was it he always felt like the older of them?

Maybe because Thomas had become a vampire when he was young. Physically he looked maybe thirty, while Rick had been closing in on thirty-five when they met.

Even so, Rick mused, you'd expect a little more maturity in a grown vampire after all those years of experience. But Thomas couldn't seem to contain himself. The vampire bounced on the balls of his feet, fairly bubbling over with eagerness while he checked out the people clustered around the bar.

He must really want a woman bad. Rick had to force himself not to be insulted by that. After all, he had as much to gain from finding the elusive woman as his partner did, maybe more. Through their recent experience when making love, for one blissful moment he'd glimpsed what could happen if they found her. Another mind to join both of theirs when linked. Someone to share control.

Still, it was only a guess that she'd show up here, in Sedilous. Were they drawing her, as she drew them? He hoped so. Given that the space station was the only neutral gathering place for two star systems—whether you were carrying legit cargo or not—it was the only logical place they could meet her but then again, that didn't mean much.

It was only a guess that her more frequent brushes with their minds meant increasing proximity. Maybe she was simply becoming accustomed to finding the mental pathway that they tapped into. She could be light-years away if her psyche was strong.

The raucous cacophony subsided, to be replaced by a short interval of sweet silence. When the speakers crackled to life once more, they emitted the wail of a saxophone and the tinkle of a piano backing a deep-voiced blues singer. Appropriate. He'd bet most of the people around him were on intimate terms with the blues.

He glanced around at the "ladies" crowding the small bar. They all failed to give off a psi signature that came anywhere close to what he'd sensed of their woman. Most of them were norms with no psi signatures at all.

One of the taller and more slender women in the group raised a glass when his gaze swept over her. Thomas nodded to her, and she sashayed between the tables.

She was pretty enough but Rick had to force himself not to recoil as she approached and her body odor filled the air round them. Dear god, what a stench. She smelled like she'd been cooped up in an escape pod with rotting livestock for a month, then showered in some cheap scent to make herself attractive. Even as eager as Thomas was, his nose wrinkled and he leaned back. Rick breathed through his mouth once and gave up. Either he'd hold his breath long enough to pass out or she'd leave.

While Rick tried not to gag, Thomas got rid of her by mumbling something and signaling the barkeep to give her a drink. It took the air a while to clear after she left. The way the other women quickly closed in around her didn't raise his hopes for their olfactory appeal.

Rick sought refuge by taking a hasty swig from his mug, wincing at the burn. It was Delion Ale, something he'd used more than once as a paint-thinner when he'd had no alternative. Here, management had watered it down to be drinkable. They diluted the blood serum and grain alcohol too, if Thomas' sour expression was any indication. The psi toyed with the idea of throwing in the towel and heading back to the *Sleepwalker*.

If their lady really did exist, she'd never show up here. This place was miserable and filthy. Definitely the last place you'd expect to see anything even close to what he wanted, a refined lady of taste and beauty.

Which was why when the chocolate-skinned woman with the golden eyes strode through the door, every man and woman in the joint riveted their attention on her. She was a lovely thing to look at, who made even her simple clothing look elegant. A long green tunic topped black leggings and high-heeled boots that made her legs look a light-year long. Even considering her dusty travel vest, she was a vision of perfection. Someone that gorgeous was completely out of place and alien to most of the bar's patrons. To them she must have appeared a dream.

To the vampire and his companion, she looked like so much more.

Harriet blinked in the gloom of Sedilous Tavern, the station's only bar. She drew in a deep breath, testing the air, and had to work not to recoil from the assorted smells that assaulted her. Fear, deception, bad booze, unwashed bodies and sex. The latter was a mingling of anticipation and the remnants of last night. All in all, not a pleasant combination.

The music throbbing from the overhead speakers was a welcome surprise. She'd expected something along the lines of an auditory assault but the smooth sounds rolled over her in a comfortable wave of memories. Her friend and co-worker Bernie always played jazz recordings in the background, even at work.

Tavern was a pretentious name. She'd rate this joint somewhere between a bare-knuckle bar and a sewer. Even in her most disreputable clothes, she stood out like a signal beacon.

Damn Chris for having her arrive at the last minute and by way of the most complicated path possible. If he'd booked her convoluted travel itinerary for any reason other than maximizing his department's budget, she'd—well, that thought didn't bear pursuing.

It wouldn't do to tear the boss apart limb by limb…much as that might be fun, she needed this job and she was damned good at it. When she was left alone to do things her way.

The deadbeats she was here to find had better show. That's all she had to say.

Her eyes rapidly adjusted to the lower light level and, breathing through her mouth, she scanned the layout first, noting exits and doorways then the patrons. The typical seedy crowd, as she'd expected. Some of them would be more—or less—than they appeared. A place like this always drew a few hiders. She'd work her way around the room and see what she could pick up.

A gal had to look out for herself. Cash for a bounty or two on the side would go a long way to easing her irritation at the detours she'd been forced to take. She could swing by an interstellar lockup on the way back and make the drop, with Chris none the wiser.

In fact, pulling one over on him would make it that much sweeter.

There was a brush against her mind and Harriet felt a strong compulsion to look in the direction of the bar. She froze.

Someone knew she was here but that wasn't surprising. The way they all stared at her, no one had failed to notice her entrance. But this was someone with strong psi powers who wanted her to look that way—his way, for there was something clearly masculine about the touch.

There was also something uncomfortably familiar about the mind…no, make that plural, because she could feel a second one. Not as powerful a psi but still distinctly the mind of a parafolk. Could be a vampire, she figured, or possibly even someone like her, if his ancestors had shared the fate of hers. Her bloodline carried a few anomalies, thanks to some imaginative genetic manipulation by unscrupulous researchers who'd gotten hold of her grandmother. Of course she'd never met anyone quite like her before, so that was pretty much out of the question.

She sniffed to see if she could separate him out of the mob and couldn't tell a thing about any individual. There were too many scents, too much clutter overloading her sense of smell. Disgusted, she resumed breathing through her mouth.

She'd bet almost anything the second mind was a vampire. Possibly even one of the marks she was looking for.

Even so, it shook her. The point remained that she'd felt that touch — or something very much like it — in the recent past. Not more than twenty-four hours ago, in fact, during her last night on the transport.

Her sleep had been disturbed by erotic images, figures locked in sensual pleasure, shadowed in gold and purple light and alive with passion. The light had drawn her, and in her dream her body had heated and thrilled as she'd watched. But then the purple began to fade and she'd found herself reaching with her mind to support it, knowing somehow that maintaining a balance was important. The purple light had flared in response and she awakened in sweat-soaked sheets. Her aching pussy had required considerable time and attention to satisfy. Unfortunately, there hadn't been a cock she was interested in anywhere in the vicinity.

Harriet pulled her mind from the past into the present. No point thinking about erotic dreams or cocks when she had work to do. Instead, she checked out the room without overtly looking in the direction that mind wanted her to look. She stifled a curse. Resisting the compulsion took more concentration than she was comfortable with.

In her peripheral vision, the gnarled barkeep polished a glass with a grubby rag. Nothing remarkable about that. She turned her head a little further. The group around the bar included a couple of men who stood out, in part for their lack of grime but also for their apparent youth. One of them, the darker of the two, fairly bounced up and down on the balls of his feet.

She turned to face them. The blond man gave her a steady stare as he picked up his glass, but the dark one smiled broadly. Even in the dim light, she made out the small sharp fangs protruding from his upper jaw.

Images from a file popped into her head, matching both faces before her. Well, well. Look what fate had dropped into her lap. Harriet enjoyed a brief moment of satisfaction, letting a welcoming smile slide onto her face.

Life was about to get a lot more profitable.

Chapter Two

෨

Thomas put his serum-nol down and stared. Without thinking, he pulled on his lower lip, revealing his fangs and licking them gingerly.

He smiled. "It's her, Rick. I just know it."

Rick didn't chide Thomas for not using their link. He couldn't help his own reaction. He picked up his glass and downed the contents in a gulp. Only after the burn hit him did he remember what it was. He coughed and gasped and had barely recovered when he noticed his vampire partner heading across the room to intercept her.

Not without him! Sudden jealousy overtook Rick and he rushed to the couple now standing in the middle of the small dance floor. The only thing he couldn't figure out was just who it was he was jealous over—Thomas or the unknown woman.

She was smiling up at his partner when he arrived. "You're a vampire? How interesting!"

Her words did not inspire Rick with confidence. *Oh God, please let her have a brain!* In spite of Thomas' many wonderful qualities, he'd never had the patience to master astrochess and Rick was tired of being beaten by the *Sleepwalker*'s AI.

Beauty she had in quantity. High cheekbones swept up under her compelling golden eyes and her skin glowed a warm deep brown. She ran her tongue over her plump lips and he imagined her opening that smile to take his cock into the heat of her mouth. A rush of desire swept through him and he jerked his attention away with an effort.

Golden streaks decorated her short, curly and otherwise near-black hair. Lovely and exotic. He'd never seen anyone with quite that coloring. He wondered if her breasts were that same shade of chocolate—oh stars, were her nipples black or pink?—and if her pussy hair was also streaked with gold.

What a contrast her skin would make, with him and Thomas being so pale! The mental image of them both riding her, one below and one above, made his cock jerk in anticipation.

His partner took her hand and made a great show of bending over it and kissing her palm. "Thomas Morelli, at your service."

Rick barely resisted rolling his eyes. Thomas could be a complete ass at times, and it looked like this was one of those times.

Whoever she was, his partner's lack of subtlety didn't appear to bother her. She hooked her arm through Thomas' and fairly purred. "Want to dance?"

Rick had no choice but to back off as the two slid into each other's arms and began to shuffle to the music. Leaning his hip on an unoccupied table, he toyed with his empty glass and fumed as they put their heads together and whispered.

Unable to restrain himself, he tightened his mental focus to eliminate any chance of his words slipping out into the crowd around them. *I thought we were supposed to share.*

We will. I'm gathering intelligence. The vampire's delighted laughter came across the link loud and clear.

Two could play at that game. Rick reached out with his mind and brushed against hers, lightly so she wouldn't notice.

He encountered shields. Very strong shields. He was unable to get even a glimpse of her thoughts.

Joy spread through him. While not a typical psi, with that strength she would be able to control the link when they fucked and Thomas fed, leaving him free to give himself over to the glorious sensations he'd had a taste of earlier. Give up completely, without fear or reservations. His cock hardened with anticipation and his pulse raced.

A rich laugh rolled out of her and across Rick's skin like warm brandy. The real stuff, not synth.

She was a beauty. She was soft in all the right places. She had a wonderful laugh.

Sure, she probably wouldn't turn out any better at astrochess than Thomas was. He'd no doubt have to continue to play the AI, who would no doubt continue to beat him.

What did it matter if she wasn't scholar material? She was far more fuckable than the computer ever would be.

I think you should stop daydreaming and cut in here.

Rick looked up to see the dancers winding down as the music faded. He set his glass down and reached Thomas and their mystery woman in one stride. "May I take a turn now?"

"Harriet, this is my partner Rick." Thomas presented her to Rick with a flourish and she grinned up at him.

"Thank you, Thomas Morelli. I enjoyed our dance."

"It was my pleasure. I hope you enjoy this dance as well."

She looked directly into Rick's eyes and her grin faded into a sultry smile. "I'm sure I will."

For a moment Harriet enjoyed eyeing Rick. A woman could drown in those ocean-blue eyes of his. She tore her gaze away and took a glance down. The man lived up to her expectations in that department as well, she thought in satisfaction. It had been clear from talking to Thomas that while he'd approached her first, they were both interested in her. Rick was packing plenty of evidence of that.

Not that Thomas wasn't adorable in a fangy, exuberant vampire kind of way. She'd always wanted her own pet bloodsucker. But even without fangs, Rick's charm was inescapable.

31

My, my, what a delicious dilemma for a woman to have — to choose between two such luscious men. The good news was that she'd picked up enough from her first dance partner's mind to know that choosing was going to be more about time and place than about whom. A delightful aroma of anticipation exuded from both of them too, overpowering the stench of their surroundings.

Movement in the shadows caught her attention. A familiar form slipped from a doorway into a seat at a table half-concealed in shadows. Her nostrils flared and she recognized a whiff of bitterness even from across the room.

Gule's fleck! What was *he* doing here?

She disengaged her hand from Rick's grasp. "Excuse me a moment, will you please?" Softening the words with a smile full of reassurance, she added, "I'll be right back. I promise."

Her anger carried her across the intervening space to where the man she'd recognized hunkered deeper into his chair, aware she'd spotted him.

She leaned over him and willed him to look up. "Giles — you bastard! This is my deal!" His shoulders hunched but he resisted her will. She pressed harder, bringing more of her personality to bear on him. "No wonder Chris booked me the itinerary from hell!"

"I-I-I-I don't know what you're talking about." The acrid scent of fear oozed from his pores, overwhelming his usual bitter odor.

"No? Well, maybe you're just here by coincidence and your gig is someone else entirely, but don't horn in on my catch. I work alone, I'm more than competent and you'd better keep out of my way. Understood?"

Thomas grabbed Rick's arm. "Isn't she magnificent? Just like Femmetal Alice."

Rick winced and pried the tight grip into a more comfortable demand on his elbow. Eying the furious woman, he considered the question. Femmetal Alice was Thomas' favorite holo-vid game action heroine. Shaped like a wet dream, skilled at anything you could think of and ready to seduce or slay at any moment. Some of their most energetic lovemaking sessions had come after Thomas spent a day accompanying Alice on her adventures.

Harriet did resemble Alice in many ways, from the thigh-high boots to her nipped-in waist. She'd altered in almost a heartbeat too, from siren to soldier. "Yeah, if you like the rough stuff."

"Gods, sometimes I do. You know?" Thomas breathed a soft sigh, and Rick could sense his arousal.

"I know. But what happened to your women-are-soft-and-cuddly argument?" As he expected, Thomas ignored him. Once his vampire partner was fixated on something—or someone—common sense tended to climb into the cargo hold.

Particularly if that someone was a woman built like his favorite holo-vid game character, all curves and tight muscles.

They watched as she leaned over the guy, pushing him farther into his seat with just her presence. The soft words the two exchanged were lost in the general noise of the bar. From the frown of concentration Thomas wore, he was trying to eavesdrop.

"Any luck?"

Thomas shrugged. "No. Too many others talking over the music."

"Wonder what he did to piss her off like that?"

"Think we ought to interfere?"

Rick shook his head. "Not until we know more. Unless I miss my guess, that guy's even more on the side of lawlessness than we are. I'm not about to step into the middle of what could be an intergalactic mob war. We're about stealth and slipping in and out unnoticed, you know?"

"I will not have this!"

Rick looked at him in surprise. Thomas didn't often speak to him in that tone.

"I will not have my companion making sense!" A grin played around his mouth. "As the older and wiser partner, I'm supposed to be in charge."

"Hey, you can be in charge," Rick assured him in a mild tone. "Just do it in a mature manner."

Thomas' face broke into a true grin. "The day I grow up will be the day you can stake me."

Rick returned his attention to their woman—realizing he'd been thinking of her in the possessive. "How much longer before he draws on her? He's packing at least one sidearm as far as I can tell."

"Hmmm...if he hasn't dropped her yet, either he knows he deserves what she's dishing out or he can't kill her, for whatever reason."

Rick strained to hear her furious soft tone, wishing her shields weren't keeping him out of their conversation. He couldn't pick up anything from her, but the man she was yelling at was giving off near-nauseating waves of fear. Unconsciously Rick slid shut his link to his more sensitive partner.

She raised her voice and Thomas reported, "She's chewing him out for being here. Says she doesn't need backup."

That last bit made Rick reassess her supposedly delicate frame and he frowned. "Sounds like she might be some kind of bounty hunter. Wonder who she's tagging?"

"In this place, could be anyone." Thomas looked around at the scattered drinkers. Every one of them watched with rapt attention as the woman hissed her fury. "Whoever it is, it isn't us. We haven't done anything to deserve that kind of attention."

"Not recently, at any rate. Lucky this run's on the up and up." Rick watched her for a moment and gave a low whistle of appreciation. "She's gotta be running out of steam by now."

"One would think."

"It's time someone rescued that poor guy. If they're not going to kill each other, she should let him go."

Thomas pushed away from the bar. "True. Besides, we're the ones who want her attention. Let's go. We'll grab her on the way out."

"Break up the two? Good idea."

Rick followed him across the room. He felt the attention of the crowd shift to include the two of them as they approached the table in the shadows.

"Hey, beautiful," Thomas said as he sidled into her field of vision. "Did you forget about us?"

Her face turned to him. Even as lightly linked as they were, Rick felt the impact of her regard like a physical blow as she stared at Thomas.

To his surprise, the man hunched in his seat spoke up. "Do I know you?"

"Now that is an interesting question. How well does anyone ever know another person?" Rick could tell Thomas worked to keep his tone light and his fangs hidden. Unthreatening.

The woman leaned over her victim. "Remember what I said, you little snot. If you step one toe out of line, you're history, connections or no connections. This is *my* gig."

Turning back to Thomas, she linked her arm through his and led the way back to the bar. "Now, you were wanting to discuss philosophy?"

"What's the story with him?" Thomas jerked his head in the direction of the shadowed table.

She made a dismissive gesture. "Enh. Long, dull story. Little man, big suit. I don't suffer fools gladly." She turned to Rick, sliding a hand around his waist to pull him along as well. "But you two definitely aren't that kind. As a matter of fact, I think you're both big men. Where it counts."

Thomas winked at Rick over her head. "We like to think so."

Rick probed the woman's mind, gently, and encountered that brick wall again. Didn't feel quite like a psychic's shields. Didn't feel like anything he'd encountered before. He took a mental step back and got a longer perspective. The green glow was definitely there, but he couldn't reach it. Somehow, she was blocking him. Was it intentional?

He'd heard mental trauma could cause complete blockage. Was this her problem? Gods, he hoped not. That would put her out of the equation he and Thomas had been hoping for.

The brick wall around her mind shimmered. A small patch thinned, revealing a stronger green glow. He moved closer and it snapped shut.

Shit! How did she do that?

He'd severed the complete link with Thomas when the waves of fear radiating from the little snot became nauseating, not wanting to inflict it on his partner. Now he strengthened it, lightly brushing against Thomas to let him know. He also began listening to the conversation, which had gone on without him.

"Your ship is that fast?" Her wide eyes and enthusiasm struck Rick as just a little overdone.

"Sure she is. You want to check her out?"

All kinds of warning bells rang in his head. Too late. Thomas had already taken the bait, steering her toward the door with the invitation.

This is not wise, he sent through their link. The original plan had included finding a room on the station. They rarely let anyone onto their ship.

Forget it, bud, this is what we came for. She is ours.

I'm not so sure about that. Something feels off about this. Who's her mark? She's probably after somebody else, but if so why is she leaving with us? What was her problem with that little guy she ripped a new one and why is she suddenly so taken with you? It doesn't add up.

Yes, it does add up. It adds up to us getting laid by a stunning woman. His tone was petulant. Rick half expected him to go on and say, "But she followed me home, can I keep her?"

He turned to the woman to find her glancing between them as if she could hear their mental conversation. Looking at her bright eyes and eager smile, Rick would never have guessed she could turn into the Bitch From Hell, the way she'd just lit into that guy. Her slender hands and manicured nails, which were right now tracing Thomas' biceps through his shirt, did not look like those of a fighter. Yet the guy in the tavern feared her. A lot, even though she admitted he had important connections.

Who the hell was she?

Even more important, *what* the hell was she? That guy had been terrified of what seemed to be a defenseless woman. He didn't really believe the defenseless part but he sure believed the guy's fear.

Rick had long ago learned that what he didn't understand could be very, very dangerous.

He and Thomas were here to refuel and get on their way. Maybe get laid at the same time. They were headed to another sector to deliver their cargo and didn't have any room in their schedule to get entangled in someone else's problems. Unless he missed his guess, this situation could turn into just that.

But there was little use arguing with his partner when he was like this. Thomas had a one-track mind when he was on the trail of pussy. With a sigh, Rick let the door swing closed behind him and followed the two on the track that led to their berth at the spaceport.

Rick had almost caught up with Thomas and Harriet when he walked into an aura of danger. Waves of anticipation, a feeling of impending violence, raised the hair on the back of his neck. He extended his senses and scanned the area, looking for a source. Could be anything from a tech chasing a baggage bot that had run off-course to a psychotic who'd gotten hold of a nerk gun. Bad things happened in spaceports.

Strange. On their way in, this area of the port had been bustling with activity. Now nothing moved.

He called out a warning to Thomas through their link, feeding him the impression as he received it.

The feeling of danger deepened and solidified, allowing Rick to locate its source. He turned his head to look. The menacing vibes came from the shadows of one of the larger vessels, a big yacht berthed near the *Sleepwalker*.

They poured out of the darkness. Humanoids. Five of them, armed with zaps. They wore half-helmets with vision shields.

Thomas' protective instincts surged through the link. Pushing Harriet behind him, he leapt between Rick and danger, eyes blazing red and canines fully on display. He grabbed the nearest hand holding a zap and shoved it to the side. Using his grip on the gun, he pulled the man to him and sank his teeth into the now terrified and struggling figure, tearing his throat out. He flung the lifeless body to one side.

Rick fell back, letting Thomas bear the brunt of the leader's charge, and waited to jam his fist with deadly accuracy into the throat of their second attacker, crushing his windpipe. Caught by surprise, the man fell without firing a blast.

In the meantime Thomas lifted the third man, broke him over his knee and tossed him on top of the second.

Three down, two to go. But he'd lost track of those two in the initial heat of battle. Fear clutching his gut, Rick frantically looked around for them.

A sharp grunt from behind caught his attention. They turned to find Harriet had become a female buzz saw, whirling kicks and punches at one of the remaining attackers. As she beat him bloody, they found her first target, slumped motionless against the yacht's landing gear.

"Sweet Sol!" Thomas exclaimed. "Where the hell did they come from?"

I want to know where she came from, Rick sent through their link. *This is getting weirder and weirder.*

Harriet knelt beside one of their attackers. She peeled back his jacket and removed a slim ID packet. "Grab their zaps."

Rick found himself following her order, gathering the scattered weapons. When he stood up with the second one in his hand, he faced Thomas, who had done the same with the other three.

Damn, they'd both complied without thinking. What the fuck was she?

"I know these guys, or at least their outfit," Harriet said as she flipped the packet closed. "They never work without backup. Good backup." She glanced back the way they'd come and seemed to come to attention as if she heard something they couldn't. "No time. We'd better run for it. How far to your ship?"

Thomas pointed to the next berth. "She's right here."

Harriet took a step toward them and cursed as she nearly tripped. She tugged off one of her boots and glared balefully at it. "I can't believe I broke my heel!" She ripped off the second one and followed them in her stocking feet, growling furiously. "They were brand new, too. Cost me an arm and a leg. Gule's fleck, what a day."

While Thomas punched in the code to open the hatch, Rick spoke through their link. *Those guys aren't pros but they're close to it. I caught their excitement and nerves just before they appeared.*

Just as I smelled their adrenaline.

She knows them. Where does that leave her?

The hatch popped open and Thomas leapt up into the airlock. "No time for the stairs." He reached to help her. "Give me your hand…"

Harriet leapt to the space beside him with ease, landing lightly at his side. After Thomas shut his dropped jaw, he joined her in giving Rick a hand, pulling him up and into the craft.

Where does that leave her? Thomas' mental voice said. *It leaves her with us. Knowledge is power.*

Damn. One way or another, Thomas was determined to keep her, whatever and whoever she was. *But we have a huge lack of knowledge when it comes to her. She knows them well enough to know they work with well-equipped backup. That puts her in their league, doesn't it?*

Let's give her a chance to explain herself, okay? There might be a perfectly innocent explanation.

And anvils might fly.

Thomas turned to glare at him and Harriet stared at both of them, a glint of humor in her expression. "What are you guys doing, talking in some private code?"

"Sort of." Rick cycled the hatch closed while Thomas went to the bridge to hail the station. The engines were already rumbling to life. "We've been together a long time."

"And he's a vampire. That probably makes you older than you look." She gave him a sharp look. "Unless he feeds elsewhere. Which I doubt, given that you're his companion."

Rick paused and gave her his full attention, again re-evaluating her. She knew far more than she should. The parafolk had a tendency for secrecy, so either she was dangerously well informed…or she was one of them.

That could be interesting. Even better, there might actually be a brain or two residing in that stunningly beautiful head of hers.

Brains, brawn *and* beauty, as well as being a strong psi? This woman was too good to be true. All of Rick's suspicions returned and went into overdrive.

He took her elbow. "Let's go to the bridge. I think we need to talk."

Harriet smiled and for the first time Rick noticed how sharp her teeth looked. Another thing to wonder about. "Perhaps we do. Lead on."

She let him keep her arm and followed him with a docility he didn't believe for an instant.

Chapter Three

ॐ

Harriet let Rick guide her to the bridge, although she could have found it without him. They followed Thomas' distinctive odor along the path he'd taken through the narrow corridor as it twisted and turned.

Once she sensed an interesting mélange of smells lingering down one of the branches that must lead to a storage hold. Some of the fainter scents were clearly identifiable as substances she knew to be illegal, at least in some parts of the galaxy.

Her info on these two wasn't at fault after all—which, she was beginning to think, was a crying shame. When she'd danced with Thomas, his mind had been open to her and she'd seen a few of his fantasies—very hot, sexy fantasies that had made her nearly squirm with delight.

Unfortunately she just wasn't comfortable with the idea of going to bed with a man right before she saw to it that he spent a very long time on a prison planet. She might tempt and tease, but she'd never seduced a target before taking him down. At least she'd never done so once she knew he was a target. There had been that one guy on Harring Seven—but this time she knew who the bad guys were and had orders to bring them in.

No, sex with the desirable vampire or his luscious companion was not in her immediate future. Oh well. Good thing she had her favorite vibrator along, safe in a pocket of her travel vest.

Don't leave home without it was her motto. Her sex toy, plus a set of spare power cells, were safely stowed right next to her stunner, which she'd had fitted with a UV light emitter, in honor of her quarry this time.

A brush of purple slid across her shields — the psi, Rick, trying again to probe her. He was a persistent one. He knew she wasn't what she seemed. She could smell his uncertainty and distrust but she knew he didn't want to act on his suspicions.

Like Thomas, he too wanted her — and in her heart of hearts, she wanted him. And Thomas.

Hmm, Tom, Rick and Harriet? That sounded like someone's idea of a bad joke. Probably just as well they weren't going to end up in bed together.

They reached the bridge just in time to hear Thomas arguing with the station's comm center. "Yes, I know we were supposed to stay until tomorrow, but we've just received an urgent message. We need to get some very important vaccine to the G-quadrant right away." He turned and rolled his eyes at them. "It's a matter of life and death."

The station's comm officer wasn't buying the story Thomas was feeding him. "Does this life-or-death matter have any relationship to the four very dead bodies we found in the berth next to yours?

Four bodies, not five? The three on the bridge exchanged concerned glances, but Harriet shrugged philosophically. The vampire's victims were surely dead and she'd seen the one Rick took down gasp his last breath. One of hers must not have been as dead as she'd thought, or else the backup she'd sensed coming had removed one of the bodies for some reason.

Maybe it had been important that one of them not be identified. She almost hoped that was the explanation, rather than that the man had crawled away. She'd hate to think she was getting sloppy. Too much time spent out of the field led to that sort of thing. Of course if she had her way, she'd be out of the field completely and happily sitting at the desk job she wanted.

Harriet wanted to howl her dismay. *The universe just wasn't fair.* But true as that was, it wasn't getting them off the space station where they'd just been attacked by some very bad guys who had even better bad guys behind them. They needed to get out of here. Now.

Thomas was using his charm on the station's comm officer over the audio link. "There were bodies outside our ship? How terrible! I'm relieved we didn't run into the killers. But we must be on our way."

"Listen, *Sleepwalker*," the comm officer sounded almost bored, "you know you can't just blast out of here like this. We've got you locked down until the murders of those men can be cleared up."

"But we don't have time to be involved. Our ship is now due into Greegan's Cross in two stellar days. It's imperative we make it there on time."

Rick was at another console, his fingers dancing over buttons and dials on a control board she wasn't familiar with. He was speaking too softly for her to make out any of the words, even with her superior hearing. After a couple of moments he looked up and nodded.

Suddenly alarms on the bridge rang out and Harriet's hands flew up to cover her sensitive ears. On every display, colored lights flashed in unison then individually, occasionally making patterns that were quite pretty, even if they made no sense whatsoever.

Thomas' smile grew until his fangs appeared. "I'm sorry, comm, but we're having some difficulties with our computers." He shouted over his shoulder. "Is it that el-ve virus again?"

Rick shouted back, his voice loud enough to be picked up by the audio-only connection to the station. "I'm afraid so. I thought it was contained, but it seems to have broken loose. We're going to have to cut comm before it gets to the station."

"A *virus*! You have virus onboard?" The station's comm officer sounded panic-stricken.

"Afraid so," Thomas' voice rang with dismay but his features contorted in an effort not to laugh. "Picked it up a few months ago and it's been a real pain. You wouldn't happen to have any scrubbing apps, would you? I'll pay top dollar for the latest updates. I'm sorry I can't monitor its activity with regard to your link, but my readouts are all whacked." He sounded convincingly apologetic and if Harriet hadn't been watching his face, she would have been convinced. "If you don't believe me, check your connections to our ship. You can read what's happening for yourself."

"One minute, *Sleepwalker*."

For a while the lights and alarms went on. Then on one of the few display boards unaffected by the colorful display, a line of red dots suddenly flashed to green. Harriet leaned over to check and saw that the docking clamps on their ship had been released.

The station's comm officer came back on the line, clearing his throat forcefully. "*Sleepwalker*, in deference to your emergency you have been cleared for immediate takeoff. Next time you want a berth with us, we will require certification that your computer systems are virus-free before you are cleared for docking. You understand, of course."

"Of course, Station Command. We'll be sure to do that. And thanks for the hospitality," Thomas told him cheerfully. He logged off. After a few more button presses and the flick of a switch, the ship drifted up and away from the dock. When Thomas punched another button, they boosted into orbit.

As soon as they were away, Rick waved his hand and the alarms cut out. "Okay, Elvie," he said. "You can quit messing with the sensors now."

A disembodied woman's voice sounded from one of the overhead speakers. "Sure, Ricky." The lights stopped their colorful dance and settled down into the usual patterns. "Nice talking our way out of there, Tommy. One more thing," she said, once things were back to normal. "I do wish you'd quit referring to me as a virus."

Harriet blinked and stared at the ceiling. "Uh, who is that?"

Thomas smiled brightly. "Elvie, our AI. She runs the ship for us. Takes care of things when we aren't here or when we're both off duty. Sometimes she'll help us out a little, like with that light display and getting the engines revved up in a hurry." He indicated Harriet to the overheard speaker. "Elvie, this is Harriet...uh, sweetheart, I didn't get your last name?"

"Lunas," she supplied automatically as dismay sped through her. "You have an AI co-pilot?" Her plan had relied on her being able to overpower the men and commandeer the ship, but there wouldn't be any way to do that with an AI in charge of the ship's operations. An integrated AI was a built-in watchdog, nearly impossible to dislodge without the appropriate tools, such as a real computer virus. Although her vest pockets carried some interesting and esoteric items, she hadn't packed anything to defeat an AI.

Christian's briefing about Thomas, Rick and the *Sleepwalker* hadn't included any of this information. In fact, there was a lot about the situation he'd dropped her into that she was beginning to question, to the point where she was wondering why she was here at all.

The gig had appeared straightforward. Take the pair into custody for back-payments on their loan and seize their ship, which they'd used for collateral. But first there was the circuitous route she'd been given to get here and the lack of guilt or pretense in Thomas' mind. Add that to the fact that Christian's toady Giles was on the scene ahead of her and a hit squad had been waiting, possibly as much for her as for them. The ID she'd grabbed from the attacker indicated he was a member of the merc guild Chris often used for aspects of the repo business that might give Galaxy Financial's shareholders indigestion.

Harriet smelled more than the usual shipboard smells or the enticingly rich smells of the men with her. She smelled a big, fat, double-crossing space-rat, one that smelled just like her boss.

Folding her arms, she stared at the pair in front of her. Rick was already somber, while Thomas' expression grew more sober all the time.

"We really need to talk," she said.

* * * * *

"...and that's it. I was sent here to confiscate your ship for missed payments and to drop you off at the nearest judicial court." Harriet finished outlining the situation while Thomas paced the room, fury in his expression. Rick sat in the seat opposite, listening to her story.

"I don't frelling believe it!" Thomas exploded. "Galaxy Financial is a well-respected institution. That's why I went there for a loan in the first place! Gods, if we can't trust Galaxy Financial, who can we trust?"

If it hadn't been such a serious situation, Rick would've laughed out loud. Thomas finished his tirade using the Galaxy slogan, and he was sure his partner had done it unconsciously.

All the money they'd paid—over how many years?— embezzled by one of Galaxy's managers. Sweet Sol, how had this Chris fellow done it?

He asked as much, adding, "Cash comes in, and there's a record of the transfer. Some of our payments, at least as long as I've been here, have been made at another bank's branch. The financial institutions that took our money and sent it to Galaxy have to have recorded the transactions. Galaxy's reputation hasn't been built on shoddy back-office operations."

"Hmmm...you have a point. If you can prove to my satisfaction that the payments have been made on time, I won't run you in. I can get access to some of our partner's records for corroboration. The big question is, are you willing to open your books to me?"

"Can you make enough sense of them to determine that? You're a bounty hunter," Rick pointed out.

"Repo officer," she corrected. "Trust me. I can run rings around either of you when it comes to financial accounting." Harriet's tone dripped ice. "I'm more than a repo agent. Much more. Now, are you going to let me see your records?"

Thomas scowled at her. "I don't see where you've left us any choice."

A disembodied voice came from the ceiling speakers. "Tommy, you're in it deep this time, aren't you?"

"Elvie," Thomas warned with an upward glance, "I'm not in the mood. If you can help, do so. If not, shut up."

"I suggest you let her see the books, pronto. The payments were made. I know. I make the transfers and enter them in your books each month."

"You hand over your financial transactions to an AI?" Harriet's tone was shocked.

"Why not?" Thomas shrugged his shoulders. "I let her run the ship when I sleep. I have her plot courses and set up itineraries. That's betting my life on her. Why wouldn't I trust her to make a few simple mathematical calculations?"

"I am fully conversant with all standard accounting principles, Hairy-It," the AI stretched out her name into what was clearly an insult. "Tommy's finances aren't that complicated. Even if they were, I have access to a wide variety of accounting texts and sample filings."

"Elvie, just give her what she needs to make her evaluation. Permit access to anything related to payment of our loan." Thomas watched Harriet's tight expression while he spoke. "Anything else she requests, ask me first."

"Certainly. I've activated the console in the lounge." Rick had never heard Elvie use that inhospitable tone before. Sure, she joked around with them, calling them her pet names, but this kind of hostility was unprecedented. Nice to know she took their welfare seriously. Unless she had a chip on her shoulder about anyone questioning the finances.

"Thank you, Elvie, and don't forget to supply refreshments for our auditor." Thomas motioned Harriet in front of him into the corridor. "Third door on the right. The second one's the head, should you need it."

Harriet's tone was just as formal but only somewhat cool. "Thank you. I'll let you know what I find out."

Tom stepped back onto the bridge and slid the door shut. "Elvie, keep an eye on her. She'll have to go through you to get any outside data. I want to know what she accesses."

"You got it, Tommy." The AI had regained her cheerfulness. "Where'd you pick up Hairy-It?"

They answered at the same time.

"In the tavern."

"On the station."

"Oh, so which was it? You two want to sync your stories? You can practice with me, but you'll have to do better than that." Elvie chuckled.

"Well, the tavern is on the station," Thomas declared.

"And you might not want to go around blathering everything you know to just anyone."

"I am not just anyone, Ricky," Elvie chided.

"I know you're not." Rick shook his head. As AIs went, she wasn't bad. He'd worked with a few bland mil-spec types and preferred her banter over strict adherence to regulations.

Thomas frowned. "Why do you call her Hairy-It? You don't like her much from your tone, but you've never given pet names to anyone but us."

"You don't know? Oh, this is sweet. Tommy, Ricky, I hate to be the one to tell you." Elvie chortled. "No I don't, I'm enjoying every minute of this. Your new friend is," she inserted a long recording of a drum roll while he and Thomas glared at the ceiling speaker, "a furry shifter. A female werewolf. To be precise, a bitch." The drum roll ended with a rim-shot.

"Well, that explains a few things," Thomas said.

Rick rubbed the bridge of his nose. "More than a few." Like her ability to resist the compulsion he had tried on her in the bar and how much her co-worker feared her. As well as how she defended herself in the ambush and then leapt up into the *Sleepwalker* without needing the stairs.

Thomas chuckled. "This is all your fault, you know." Rick looked over and he said with a grin, "It was your idea for us to get a dog."

Rick settled for rolling his eyes. "Don't be stupid enough to say that in front of her. On the other hand, I inherit everything, don't I? Okay, be as stupid as you usually are."

The toothy grin grew wider, fully exposing every fang. "Hey, you want to face all these problems by yourself? Looks like your inheritance is shrinking by the minute."

"There's this weird psi thing going on with her," Elvie continued. "I can't tell exactly what because she's got heavy shields, but whatever's behind them is strong. Maybe even stronger than you, Ricky."

Rick and Thomas stared at each other blankly.

"But what I want to know is, why did you bring her back here? She's gunning for you, and you both walked right into it."

"I thought something was up, and I tried to warn you," Rick said to Thomas. "But would you listen? No way. You smelled pussy and you went for it. We'll be lucky if we get out of this without jail time, let alone keep our ship."

"Oh wait a minute," Elvie interrupted. "She's asking for a secure long-range connection. I'll try to scoop her passwords."

"No, Elvie, don't you dare. That's what she'd expect of us if we were criminals. Let her run her data search and keep all recordings off unless she asks you to make copies." Thomas slumped back in his chair. "We need to be squeaky clean."

Rick watched his companion close his eyes and drop his head back in fatigue. "Has anyone noticed the irony of this happening on the only run I can recall when we're carrying no contraband at all, not even a secret data chip?"

"Yes. It's not lost on me." Thomas opened one eye. "From now on, we're always going to have something in the smuggler's box. If I'm going down, it's going to be for something I did, not something I didn't do. And we may need the added profits, if we have to change banks. Galaxy Financial is everywhere, and if you go through them to another institution, as a non-customer, they charge enough fees to choke a black hole."

"Oh and speaking of smuggling, George had a cargo, no questions asked, for transport. I thought we might be able to pick up double pay on this run, but it's got to be delivered out past Cumin."

Thomas closed his eye. "Short run. Too bad we're on a tight schedule here. What else did he want?"

"You ought to pay attention when people talk. You might be dangerous if you did." Rick recited, "High-quality emeralds, sterile manufacturing tips and the source of black-market lab animals."

Thomas shrugged. "Nothing on that list we're likely to run across."

Rick stood and stretched. "You may be tired, but I've got some nervous energy to work off. Weren't you looking forward to a good fuck tonight?"

Thomas watched him with one eye for a moment. Rick deliberately bent forward and flexed. He could feel the vampire's complete attention on his ass. His cock stirred as Thomas leapt to his feet and reached out to palm Rick's scrotum through his pants.

"I get to be on top tonight!"

He agreed and let Thomas hustle him off the bridge. He frog-walked along as his cock hardened and his anus tingled in anticipation. Thomas still held his balls in a firm grip.

Okay, so things weren't working out quite the way they'd hoped for when they met Harriet in the bar, but at least they had each other.

Elvie's snicker followed them down the corridor, switching speakers as they moved along. As the door slid closed behind them, she called out, "Have a ball, boys!"

Chapter Four

ಐ

The chrono showed it was well into third shift when Harriet finally closed the last file of Thomas and Rick's records. She stretched her stiff back and pondered the ramifications of the data she'd sorted through.

They'd told her the truth.

Every number checked out, from the recording of each transfer, the amount, right through the subsequent deduction of funds from their Galaxy Financial accounts. The guys had made the payments on their loans, every single one of them, never short or late and sometimes even a little ahead of schedule. In fact, twice they'd double-paid, according to the notes appended to the transactions, to pay down the loan and get out of debt a little faster.

Everything checked out, including the response tags showing the transfers had gone to Galaxy Financial's Loans Division and crediting what seemed to be the correct account. The only trouble was that the data on her minidisk, copied directly from the Loan Division records, showed no sign that those transfers ever occurred.

She even logged in through a secure comm link, using Giles' sign-on, to check the latest updates to the system. Let Chris beat him up for snooping. No one knew she had most of the password/ID combos for her department.

No dice. The two systems were irreconcilably out of balance. She even did a little research into where the money had gone and came up empty. When she tried to follow the trail of transfers she hit a brick wall. For each payment over the past twenty-three months, the appropriate amount went out of the *Sleepwalker*'s account and the accompanying notation stated it went to pay the loan. The Loan Division had no record of ever receiving it.

She didn't have clearance to access more detailed data. Chris did but, like all department heads, he used a dongle, a coded wand used to verify identity. Not only didn't she have access to a system with the required insertion port for the wand, he kept his locked up. She'd never even gotten a good look at it.

The records on the *Sleepwalker* showed the money had been paid…Galaxy's statements showed it hadn't. Her employer's records also noted that, as was usual with delinquent accounts, several warnings had gone out as a result. The *Sleepwalker* logs showed no such messages had been received.

It was like the two sets of records existed in completely different dimensions and she couldn't reconcile them at all. When an account was a few cents out of balance, she'd learned early on that it was a sign of something wrong. Sloppy bookkeeping at best, an attempt to conceal criminal acts at worst. When the discrepancy was of this magnitude, red lights went on and warning sirens blared. One of the logs was wrong, but how could she tell which one? There had to be an answer somewhere.

For a moment she wondered if there was something she'd missed, but quickly dismissed it. After all, she was a much better accountant than anyone had ever given her credit for.

After getting her basic degree in accounting, she'd earned an advanced degree in interstellar economics and there was no reason she shouldn't be able to use it. But every time she put in for a transfer to accounting, actuarials or even intersystem economic analysis, management's response was how much she was needed doing field work. Just because she had strength, agility and speed superior to normal humans, not to mention highly developed hearing and a terrifically keen sense of smell.

Hell, those weren't any more her fault than her psi powers were. All her extra genetic material was due to heredity, plain and simple, and there wasn't a damned thing she could do about it.

But that didn't matter to The Powers That Be. As far as they were concerned, she couldn't be the accountant she'd always known she was born to be, all because her parents were werewolves and because her poor grandmother had been altered into a psychic werewolf at that.

Trouble was, just because she turned furry once in a while, no one took her brains seriously.

Another thing occurred to her. Why had a delinquent account gone for that long without triggering a visit from a branch rep, or at least direct real-time communication? Thomas and Rick were in and out of local Galaxy branches all the time, making deposits, transfers and payments, yet none of their accounts had ever been flagged for personal notification of the delinquency. And there were other accounts in the *Sleepwalker*'s portfolio.

She swiftly called up images of the original loan agreement and discovered that one of those, the primary pooled investment account, was earmarked for backup transfers. The account held enough to cover a number of regular payments yet it had never been debited. She checked the links between accounts and discovered the trigger association, the notation that would enable the transfers, had never been set up in the system.

Or else it had been erased. She'd give good money to get a look at a three-year-old backup to find out which was the case.

Curiouser and curiouser. No way were Galaxy's back-office operations that sloppy. No single account could be this screwed up by accident. She didn't believe in coincidence and the money paid on the loan had to go somewhere. When she found the money, she'd find the perp. Or perps. This was looking bigger—and more serious—all the time.

Unfortunately, she'd never find the money from the depths of space, and not with the low-level access codes she had. Until she knew a lot more about what was shaping up to be a conspiracy and who was involved, she couldn't just walk into a Galaxy branch, identify herself and use their system.

Admitting defeat, Harriet logged off and rose from the galley table she'd claimed as her desk. She stood and stretched, relishing the pop of each tendon and muscle. She was tired but also tense, and needed some way to relax. Her two favorite methods for that were exercise and sex, not necessarily in that order.

It occurred to her that the guys weren't turning out to be the marks she'd thought and if she wanted, she could fuck them without guilt. Oh yeah, she wanted but she needed to sort some things out before she took that step. There were too many unanswered questions, which left a long workout as the best physical release.

Trouble was she didn't know where the ship's gym was, or if they even had one, and she didn't want to ask Elvie for that information. The AI had been frosty from the beginning and downright snippy when she'd requested the secure comm link.

Still, she had to find a place to sleep and might as well ask about the gym as well.

Clearing her throat, Harriet spoke to the ceiling as she'd noticed Thomas and Rick do when they wanted to talk to the AI. "Elvie? I'm done for now—"

"And now you want a place to sleep?" the AI interjected, not giving her a chance to finish her sentence.

"Well, yes."

"I've cleared out cabin three for your use. *As instructed.*"

The emphasis the AI put on the last phrase made it clear that Elvie had been ordered to make up Harriet's room and had under protest. Probably if the AI had her way, Harriet would spend the night sleeping on the narrow bench in the galley.

Hell, she might as well be polite, even if Elvie wasn't going to be. "Thank you, Elvie. If you'll tell me how to find it—"

Again Elvie interrupted. "The cabins are one level up. You can take the lift or use the stairs. Cabin three is the third...that is, the second door to the right. The door isn't locked, you can go right in."

The correction and sudden smugness in the computer's voice raised Harriet's suspicions, but she was too tired to care. She stumbled for the narrow circular stairs that connected the levels, went up and found the designated door.

Well, that would teach her to ignore her instincts. The second door to the right did not admit her to the empty cabin she'd been assigned. It led to another cabin, one very much filled by her hosts. In the hours she'd been occupied with the accounts Rick and Thomas had apparently been occupied with each other, from the heavy smell of sex hanging in the room, and in post-coital bliss had fallen dead asleep.

For a moment Harriet was too startled to shut the door and so she watched the pair. They lay sprawled across the bed, naked, their arms around each other, all tangled pale limbs. Rick was the bigger one, his shoulders broader than the more slender Thomas.

They looked—happy she supposed was the best way to put it—even in sleep. Like lovers did. Her heart ached as she took in the sight, knowing how long it had been since she'd slept that way with anyone.

Retreating, she closed the door and tried the next one, which Elvie had originally mentioned as being hers. She supposed the AI had been making a point, that Thomas and

Rick didn't really need her for sex...after all, they had each other.

Well, at least she had her vibrator. A poor substitute for a hot cock and not as large as she'd like, but at least it never disappointed her.

The light from the hall wasn't all that bright but it disturbed Thomas anyway. When he was in space like this, too far from a solar system to be in true vampire bondage to the sun, his sleep cycle was more or less like any other man. When not knocked out by the sun's proximity, he slept lightly.

The door closing brought him fully awake, as well as the lingering scent of a woman...okay, a werewolf, but still a female, and one who was aroused.

He couldn't help his grin. Even after an extended session of making love with his companion, an aroused female werewolf was well worth waking up for. Careful not to disturb Rick, he slipped out of the bed and found his robe.

Pausing in the hall outside her door, he heightened and extended his senses, seeking information about her. Heartbeat was raised, as he'd expected. Now that he knew what to look for, he could tune into the tell-tale signs that indicated she was a shape shifter. The idea that she could turn furry wasn't a complete turn-off for him, though. Quite the opposite. Her arousal-scent was intriguing and Thomas never could resist a challenge. Wrap sex up in it and he was so ready. For an instant he wondered what werewolf blood tasted like and if she'd let him bite her.

Of course she might toss him out of her cabin altogether.

Her heartbeat and breathing revved up suddenly. He frowned and concentrated harder on her life signs. Yes, she was definitely agitated. What could cause that? Was she frightened? Could something have slipped into her cabin? They didn't have anything toxic in their cargo, but they'd picked up unwanted passengers before while they were docked, mostly rats and snakes.

Maybe Elvie was playing a trick on her…he should check and make sure she was okay.

He opened the door just in time to hear a low feminine moan of pleasure as well as a harsh buzzing sound. Harriet lay on the bed, wearing only a thin undershirt. She was bare below the waist. He sensed the residual heat coming off the rest of her clothes, thrown onto the small cabin's only chair.

The buzzing noise came from the small rod she held against her privates, rubbing it there with urgent deliberation. Where'd she gotten hold of a vibrator?

Thomas stared as Harriet made another moan, obviously lost in the moment. He wasn't sure he'd ever seen a woman look so beautiful, with her kinked black and gold hair spread across the pillows and her face flushed with excitement. Her generous breasts strained against her shirt, the nipples hard through the fabric. He sucked in a deep breath. The smell of her sex was heavy in the air, an enticing perfume unlike any other. He inhaled again. Pussy. There was nothing like it, and hers smelled better than any other he'd come across.

Thomas' cock, which had up until that moment been relatively content, hardened for action. He considered giving it a stroke or two while watching Harriet pleasure herself.

But something must have given him away, most likely his smell since he doubted she could have heard his slow breathing over the vibrator. She opened her eyes and sprang to her feet. As he watched, her fingers lengthened, bent and curled, the nails extending into razor-sharp claws.

The anger and surprise in her scent almost overpowered her sexual excitement. Almost. He crossed his arms and smiled at her. "Looks like Elvie was right. You are a werewolf."

Eyes that had first glittered metallic-gold with passion now darkened in fury. "So my secret's out. I might have known the electronic bitch would tell on me. Don't you believe in knocking?"

"I heard something and wanted to be sure you were all right. Besides, you didn't knock when you opened my door." He let his gaze rove over her abundant breasts. With each agitated breath she took, those luscious globes quivered beneath the taut fabric. Sweet Sol, he wanted to cup them in his hands.

"I didn't mean to bother you. I was misinformed about the location of my room."

He believed her and let that thought reach her. Elvie had clearly been up to some tricks with respect to Harriet. Thomas guessed she was just jealous of the idea of "her" males taking a flesh-and-blood female onboard.

It didn't matter to him. He loved Elvie but a man couldn't fuck a computer. She'd always be an inviolate virgin as far as he was concerned.

His cock bobbed toward the woman he could have, should he be able to talk her into it. He managed to hold still while she looked him over. She took her time, examining every inch of him, spending a lot of time eyeing his erection.

Patience paid off. The claws finally retracted and the scent of her musk changed. He breathed deeply of the mix, a lingering trace of alarm spicing her arousal.

Harriet stepped closer to him. He was mesmerized by the dark nipples pearled beneath her shirt. Gods, she was gorgeous in every way that counted. Like the hair on her head, her pubic hair was black streaked with gold. The mass of curls hid her precious pussy from him. He ached to spear his tongue into her and taste her.

"Why don't you?" Harriet's question was more of a challenge.

He realized he'd been broadcasting his thoughts. Elvie had said the woman was a psi with surprising strength but something strange too. Ah what the hell, he'd worry about that later. Rick had taught him the benefits of a psychic lover. If she could hear his thoughts, it would save them both time and effort. Nothing like just thinking about what you want and having your lover respond.

She fell back onto the bed and spread her legs in obvious invitation. He forgot about Elvie and psi powers and anything but the rich perfume that enveloped him as he knelt to worship her pussy. And the taste, oh gods, the taste of her was divine. He parted the springy curls that hid her nether lips with his hands and thrust his whole face into her, as much as he could.

This was what he wanted. This was what was missing from his life with Rick. Pussy. Sweet, divine, tasty pussy.

She was soft, her skin the color of garnets as she swelled under his touch. She was the most incredible woman he'd ever tasted. He found her clit and swirled his tongue around the erect flesh. Her moan was more heartfelt than the response she'd made to the vibrator.

As if a vibrator could be a better lover than he was.

"Not a chance, Thomas."

His head jerked up and he grinned toothily. "I would hope not. Now hold on and I'll really show you something."

And he did. Harriet wasn't a quiet lover by any means and she proved to be very responsive. In moments he had her screaming his name. Or someone's name. Funny thing, he thought he heard what sounded a lot like "Rick" come out of her mouth once or twice, although she'd covered it up quickly both times.

Maybe she had a thing for his companion too. That could work out nicely, even if she didn't realize it yet.

Suddenly eager for putting something other than his tongue into her pussy, he pulled back and leaned over her. Harriet glanced at his cock. "Don't you want me to go down on you?"

Thomas grinned down at her. Oral sex he'd had plenty of, hours ago as well as for the last thirty years. Right now, he wanted pussy. Werewolf pussy. Her pussy.

He fitted his cock to her aforementioned anatomy. "Maybe later. I can't wait for this." Slowly he started to push inside.

Stars! She was hot and tight and he wanted to howl as he entered her. Hot and tight and, oh gods, her muscles clenched down along his entire length as he eased inside. Stake him if it didn't feel completely different from an asshole.

He slowed down his entry, enjoying the difference. Apparently he slowed down too much because suddenly there was a claw in his ass, not quite digging in but making her wishes felt.

He got the point. The werewolf was eager for action and unwilling to be patient. Fine, he'd indulge her. He'd do just about anything for her at this juncture.

Even speed up. Thomas put some muscle into it. Usually he had to be careful while making love, even with Rick, because his strength made it possible to hurt his partner. But he realized Harriet wasn't just any lover. She could take his full strength and then some. Something inside Thomas relaxed at that thought and he pistoned faster, enjoying the way she clutched at him.

Harriet acted like she enjoyed it too. She screamed and cried and gave a few near howls as they fucked for the first time. The noises she made spurred him on, increasing his excitement and wringing moans and growls from his throat. Sometimes he really hated how quiet Rick was when they made love.

Not that he was making comparisons between them. After all, both of them were really great in bed. They were just different.

Another difference he noted was that when he got hungry, it wasn't as easy to ask for the blood he needed.

Fucking always made him bloodthirsty, but Harriet hadn't made love with someone like him. As the thirst came over him, he wondered if she would let him bite her. He knew how to make it part of the process...even an enjoyable part, but he was reluctant to bring it up.

What do you want, vampy?

The question took him so much by surprise that he actually answered it. *I need blood...when I make love.*

Sounds kinky. So what's stopping you?

Nothing, now. Thomas dug his fangs into her neck, finding the vein and sucking hard. Harriet gasped but turned her head to give him better access. She was hot and spicy, and the wash of her blood across his tongue gave him an unexpected boost of energy.

Within moments his climax rose and it was all Thomas could do to avoid finishing before her. Fortunately, Harriet quickly reached her peak as well. She wrapped her long legs around his waist, capturing him in an intense grip, and again her fingers lengthened into claws that dug into his backside. Good thing he had a tendency to heal fast or he'd carry those marks for a long time.

Not that he minded getting a few marks from her. The way he felt right now, he'd welcome anything she did to him!

A green glow touched his mind. *You've had enough. Stop feeding.*

He did at once, sealing the marks in her neck just as Harriet cried out and climaxed again beneath him. Her cries were long and loud, and once more Thomas thrilled at her response. It was great being with a woman so ready to please.

But now he had his own orgasm to deal with, just as potent as the ones he'd had earlier with Rick. Perhaps not quite as poignant...after all, this woman was still pretty much a stranger to him and making love with someone you cared about certainly was better than someone you didn't know very well.

But as Harriet's pussy clenched tight around him and drove him completely wild with her whole-hearted participation in their lovemaking, Thomas recognized something profoundly important.

This wasn't going to be a one-time thing. Harriet was going to be part of his life forever.

He broadcast, *I'm coming!*

Harriet gathered him into a closer embrace. *So come. I'll be here for you.*

And she was, holding him in her arms and in her pussy. She pulsed her inner muscles, gripping him in a tightening sheath that plunged him over the edge at warp speed. When the last wave of passion left him, she still held him close, nuzzling his neck. Her claws gently raked his back.

He nipped her on the neck and was rewarded with her digging harder into his skin. "Be nice or I'll dump you out of the bed."

Thomas settled into her side and pulled her into his arms, letting her head rest against his shoulder. She stiffened for a moment, as if unfamiliar with this aspect of the ritual of lovemaking, but then relaxed into him.

"I guess you're into cuddling," she told him, but there wasn't more than a fleeting teasing note in her voice.

Thomas kissed her neck, being certain he'd erased all signs of his feeding. No point in making Rick more upset than he was going to be by having her carry companion-style marks. Truth was, cuddling was his favorite part of sex…well, after sex itself.

"You bet," he told her.

Chapter Five

ℬ

Thomas?

The wall chrono beside the door showed the same readout it had for months. Thomas made a mental note to have Elvie see what was wrong with it before he rolled over and found Harriet still sound asleep beside him. Unlike Rick, she'd not sprawled with him the way he liked. He supposed trust took some time to build, but last night had certainly been a good start.

He responded to Rick, opening the link fully and showing him Harriet's magnificent body spread out on the mattress. *She's fabulous, Rick. And she's all ours.*

Ours means both of us, as in we share. Rick's tone of thought was tart. A little peeved at being left out. Maybe something else. Abruptly Thomas remembered how cautious Rick had been about her. He was probably still suspicious.

We will share her, eventually. She blundered into our cabin last night and disturbed me, so I followed her to make sure she found her bed safely. His response sounded defensive, even to himself. It had started innocently enough. What did he have to be defensive about?

Good question. Got an answer for me?

Something really was wrong with his partner and it was more than Thomas getting first crack at their woman. *What time is it?*

Rick's sigh came through the link. *Time to be up and about. We've got to find out what she turned up last night and where we go from here. Does she believe we're innocent?*

Thomas regarded the still form beside him and tried not to think that she might have treated him to a pity fuck, one last fling before he went to prison. *Hard to tell. It's not like we did much talking.*

You're such a hound. I'm on my way to the mess. Meet you in a few minutes, once I have my morning brew.

Rick sounded more like himself, less grumpy, as the link faded into a background awareness. Thomas figured he'd take his time, let the caffeine mellow his companion out before he faced him. Really, he didn't have anything to worry about, did he?

Well, nothing unless his partner had taken a dislike to Harriet to the point of not wanting her around. Even after only one night with her, Thomas knew she was the woman he wanted to have in his bed and his life. But he wanted Rick there too.

Somehow he'd have to overcome any problems between them. It should be pretty easy to do…after all, they both had so much in common.

Him.

* * * * *

Harriet described every step she'd gone through, looking again for anomalies and any possibility that the system had been compromised. "None showed up. Every transfer was processed by a different clerk. The problem has to be internal and was done with some purpose. So I believe you," she stated as she grabbed the proffered mug of java from Rick's hand.

"What remains to be explored are the implications of that, for all of us, and just what we can do about it." She looked across the narrow table into Thomas' hard eyes. She couldn't blame him for being pissed off. She'd like to take a large bite out of someone's hide herself.

Geez, this was going to make a mess one way or another. Her job was basically history unless she could somehow prove that Chris had diverted the funds. And that he'd set up the ambush on Sedilous with the intent of killing her.

"What's going to happen when you don't show up as planned to turn us and our ship over to the authorities?" Rick sipped his java and stared up at the ceiling. "Or are they going to try to intercept you again?"

"Who were those assassins after, her or us?" Thomas asked quietly.

"That's the question, isn't it?" Rick cleared his throat. "Until we know the answer to that, we don't know how to proceed."

Harriet sat up straighter. "I'm not so sure we need to know." She dipped her finger in the coffee and ran a finger across the table. "If this is the line separating the pros and cons of acting in ignorance, we have on the con side, what?"

"Playing it safe."

Rick snorted. "You're not serious, are you?"

Thomas wore a sly grin. "No, but it was the only reason I could think of that we might not want to be proactive."

Harriet looked from one to the other. "Anything else?"

Both men shook their heads.

"Okay, on the pro side, what do we have?"

"Not being a stationary target." Rick leaned forward over the table, making a mark with a finger dipped in his drink, on the side she indicated. "Not getting caught off-guard again. Taking the fight to them—let's break their furniture, not ours." He made two more marks.

"Whoever they are," Thomas added.

"Right. Whoever they are." Harriet thought for a moment. How much should she reveal? Who knew just how far the conspiracy penetrated within the company? Taking on her former boss was one thing, but to chuck it all, go up against the entire weight of Galaxy Financial and throw her lot in with these rogues, was another. Did she really want to burn her bridges? On the other hand, the mercs on Sedilous had pretty much burned them for her.

Hard to be loyal to a company that was out to kill you. That pretty much sent the great benefits plan up in smoke, along with her fully vested pension. "I've got a good idea who's behind this and how it was done but to obtain proof I need access to a higher level of security clearance than I have now. I'll bet I know where I can get that, but it's a gamble and a risky act."

"Oh I like risk." Thomas sat forward, a definite gleam in his eyes. "What do we have to do?"

"We need to break into my boss's home."

Their eyebrows rose, almost disappearing into their hair. "Care to explain?" Both looked surprised that they spoke in unison. They'd been together long enough that they didn't always need to communicate silently.

She took a moment to organize her thoughts. "The transfers go out of your account in transactions that appear to be properly labeled. They clearly aren't going into your account at Galaxy. The last credit on the books is one you paid almost two years ago, from a branch in Cooter's Beach, in the Burrell System. I noticed a discrepancy in the account numbers in the notations, one that changed just after that credit. One of the sixteen digits in the loan number is wrong, a six instead of an eight. However, when I try to call up the records for that account, I can't.

"My security clearance isn't high enough, which tells me it's most likely the account of a company officer or a very important customer. However, that's all I could find out. I couldn't get even an account summary, which should give me a current balance, the account name and the managing loan officer. That much is supposed to be available to every investigator, including repo officers like me, but no dice. I tried every trick I could think of, and I can't call up anything at all that's helpful."

She took a deep breath. "Given Giles showing up on Sedilous and the ID I took off the merc, Christian is in this up to his eyeballs. He's got to be either the account manager or the account holder for the bogus loan. If I can get into my boss's house, I should be able to find either the account records or his log-on information. Maybe both."

Rick looked troubled. "We've got cargo for the colonists on Deltan and had planned to swing by The Caverns to pick up some packets for transfer to Baron's Folly on the way back. Our schedule was to rendezvous with the Baron in nine days, right after we leave Deltan. We're a little ahead of schedule, given our hasty departure from Sedilous." Rick palmed his eyes.

Of the two of them, he looked the worse for wear. But then, she was pretty certain the vamp had fed twice the night before. Speaking between his wrists, he asked, "Given that itinerary, how far out of the way does he live?"

"I was thinking of searching his second home first, which is on one of the moons in a system just this side of The Caverns. It's closer and it should be safer because he doesn't spend much time there. His wife doesn't like being that far out of civilization. She only lets him go a few times a year, for what he calls his 'solitude stays'. If he is masterminding this operation, it's likely he's in the office. Easier to keep an eye on things, especially if he's using Galaxy resources. That gives us a better chance of getting in and out unnoticed."

"Not a bad plan," Rick said. Harriet thought he sounded reluctant to give his approval. "Given our combined skills, we should be able to avoid detection."

"Ah, just what are our combined skills?" Harriet asked. "I know mine, but what are yours?"

"Well, my sense of hearing and smell are better than average." Thomas glared at her snort. "That might be redundant given you're on the team but my night vision is more acute than yours. For dogs, I know vision is their fourth-best sense."

Supercilious vamp. Claws dug into her palms, despite her efforts to control the anger that rippled across her skin. "I am not a dog," she said with deadly seriousness.

"I know you're not, darlin', but you must admit you have many shared physical characteristics."

"My psi powers are considerable," Rick hurried to add. "I can detect unshielded norms at a good distance, even through dampening fields."

Harriet smiled tightly into his intense blue eyes and willed the anger away. The vamp was poor at controlling his emotions but that was no reason for her to fail to harness hers.

"Thomas and I are stronger than norms," she said. So they had the physical angles covered. "Anyone got any electronics ability?"

The overhead speaker crackled to life. "I do, Hairy-It." Harriet bridled at the AI's abuse of her name but said nothing.

Oblivious to her anger, Elvie went on. "Let me interface with most any system and I can tie it in knots. You're talking household security here, right?"

"Maybe more than that, if this guy is running a skimming operation," Rick pointed out.

"I'd suspect it might go deeper than just funds diversion," Harriet said, "if he was willing to kill one or all of us. You might run into heavy private security. I doubt he'd have access to anything mil-spec, at least not the latest versions."

"That shouldn't be a problem," the AI told them smugly. "Just in case, I'll work on downloading the latest countermeasures. By the time we get there, I'll be up to speed on everything I can locate."

Harriet looked at Rick. From what she could tell, he was the brains of this operation, or at least the most level head.

"Elvie is well-versed in security. You might say it's her hobby. She picks up odd programs and techniques wherever she can. We don't ask and she doesn't tell us where she gets them. She's proven she's worth her weight in gold many times over."

"Tommy, that's not very flattering. You forget that I'm a series of electrons and impulses, and as such my weight is insignificant."

"It's a figure of speech, Elvie. We treasure you in whatever form you are. I think of you as beautiful sparkles of light, gleaming brighter than the purest diamond."

"Aww, Tommy, thanks. I love you too."

"Was that 'you two' or 'you too'?" Rick asked. "Am I included in this whatever-it-is, while you both are wallowing in mutual expressions of affection and goodwill?"

"Ricky, of course I love you too." Elvie simpered. Harriet thought she might gag. "I have a line on a new series of protocols. Downloading now. Updating our timetable—plan for our arrival at Willing Park in less than sixteen hours."

Harriet stood and stretched. "That gives me time to work out and catch up on my sleep. I didn't get quite as much as I was hoping for last night," she added at Rick's snort and the vampire's sudden blush. "If you'll point the way to the gym?"

"Floor below this one, in empty cargo hold three," Rick's clipped tones told her.

After she'd left, Thomas turned on his partner. "You could have been a little more pleasant, given how she's on our side now."

Rick held up his hands. "Hey, I made her coffee."

"I didn't see how Ricky was being unpleasant," Elvie broke in.

Thomas snarled at the AI. "No, you wouldn't. After all, you keep calling her Hairy-It. I've had it with both of you being rude to her. She's a good woman."

"Good in bed you mean," Elvie said.

"Not that I'd know anything about that," Rick added with a glower.

"Is this because she and I made love last night?" Thomas was incensed. "It just happened — and probably wouldn't have if Elvie hadn't sent Harriet to the wrong room and I wasn't such a light sleeper."

"I did no such thing —" Elvie began.

"Of course you did. But it didn't have the result you wanted. It just brought us together sooner."

"So that's the way it is?" Rick said. "She's really gotten to you so quickly?"

"I like her. I maybe even love her. That's what she means to me."

"That's rushing to judgment after just part of one night. Is she worth upsetting everything we have together?" Rick asked.

Thomas stared at him. "That's not my intention and you know it."

Rick glared back. "I'm not sure I do, Thomas. I've never had to share you with anyone before, not this way, and I don't think I like it." He turned and stalked out of the room before Thomas could say anything more.

"Well now, that didn't go so smoothly," Elvie said brightly. "Maybe you should rethink this werewolf fixation of yours."

"Elvie, I think you should mind your own electronic business," Thomas told her. "Do what you do best and I'll take care of my relationship issues."

He left the bridge and headed for his room. He needed a shower and space to think. There had to be a way to get things worked out between Harriet and Rick before they reached her boss's home sweet home away from home.

The plan came to him just before the automatic shutoff of the hot water forced him out of the spray. Thomas grinned. There was the possibility that it wouldn't work out, but hey, how much worse could things get?

Harriet finished her hundredth repetition on the arm-metal-flex, a strength-building machine that used resistance rather than weight to exercise muscles. It was state of the art, designed for use in low gravity conditions, such as on a ship in deep space.

She might have known these men would have the best equipment available to work out with. Everything she'd seen on the ship and in their records indicated a dedication to quality.

It made her presence there a little awkward. They obviously had very good taste…so what were they going to do with an off-bred werewolf bitch?

Well, Thomas at least could do anything he wanted. Last night's fuck had been more than just good sexual exercise. She'd realized about halfway through that there was far more than just physical interest on his part. That business of linking minds during sex left a person very open.

Thomas' thoughts were straightforward. He wanted her, not just for a simple night of sex to relieve tension but for something likely to last a lot longer.

A relationship, much like what he had with Rick.

So where did that leave her with Rick? Hard to say. According to what she'd picked up from Thomas, the tall blond wanted her too, but she'd seen no evidence of that today. He'd been irritated with her and with Thomas, even though the pair of them had been partners for decades, according to their records.

Harriet sighed and mopped the sweat off her brow before moving to another machine, this one to exercise the legs. She set it to the highest level and started her reps.

This business with the two men bothered her more than she liked. She didn't want to come between them, even if she was falling for one of them.

Her superior sense of smell caught Rick's presence even before she heard him. She turned to see him standing near the entrance, dressed as she was for exercise in a tight tank top and shorts. He was all man, tight abs, bulging arms and leg muscles, and in spite of her misgivings about the man, her mouth watered at the sight. She wondered if his body could possibly be as perfect as it looked.

"I thought you'd be done by now. You've been down here almost an hour." His voice was brusque, but the heated stare he was giving her in her gear made her wonder if he wasn't having thoughts similar to her own.

Her nipples tightened against her tank top. The next set moved the fabric across the sensitive tips, enough to make her shiver at the sensation. She had to work to return her attention to the conversation.

"Sorry. It takes longer for me to get enough reps to make the muscles burn."

Rick glanced at the setting on the arm machine and she saw his eyes widen…just a little. She'd pushed it to the top and still had to go to a hundred to get a burn.

He gave a small smile. "Not even Thomas has to top these out. I guess we'll just have to get some bigger machines…if you're going to be with us long."

She knew he could have made the comment out of politeness. Exercise was essential in space or muscles atrophied in the lower gravity of some freighters like the *Sleepwalker*. She needed machines that went higher than normal to stay healthy. She needed to use them longer than normal to keep her edge. Both Thomas and Rick showed evidence of serious gym time, so they knew why it was necessary.

It wasn't like he cared for her health all that much. He was just being polite.

Now if only he'd stop staring at her breasts, she could believe what she was telling herself about his lack of interest. She stuck her chest out further to give him more to stare at.

Rick's eyes narrowed as he apparently realized what she'd done. "You think you're pretty cute, don't you?"

She couldn't help but tease him with a cheeky grin. "I know I am. Does that bother you?"

She saw the instant Rick's temper snapped. He leaned over where she was lying on the machine, forcing her onto her back and caging her with his arms. "You're physically stronger than I am, seem to have psychic powers to rival mine and are smarter than you look. In addition, you're a beautiful woman who has my partner wrapped around her little claw."

Her breath stuttered as she inhaled the scent of him, anger combined with arousal, topped with a dollop of uncertainty. A heady mixture. The sheer potency of it made her head swim. She strove to maintain eye contact.

"He told Elvie and me to back off on you…I've never seen him take to a woman the way he has you, not in more than thirty years. So yeah, you bother me, Harriet. Maybe you are on the level, but if you aren't, you stand a very good chance of hurting someone I love."

Rick had her trapped on the bench. She could have pushed him away and freed herself easily. The strength was in her to do it, and she knew he knew that too.

He could have backed off but he didn't. She could have made him do so, but she didn't. It became a stalemate, Rick daring her to use her strength while she dared him to keep her prisoner.

Between them the tension rose until Harriet wondered if this confrontation would end in a serious fight. Or a serious kiss. Either was possible. Given his antagonism and her inner turmoil, either was likely.

Finally it was Rick who gave up. He pushed himself away and backed toward the door. "I'll come back after you finish up."

Harriet lay on the bench for long moments after he was gone, getting her raging heartbeat back to normal. And her hormones.

* * * * *

Dinner was a somber and uncomfortable affair. They ate in the small galley, Harriet squeezed in next to Thomas, Rick opposite them at the small table. Thomas sipped some kind of liquid, most likely serum, she figured, while the other two ate. Every once in a while the vampire would put a reassuring hand on Harriet's knee while she ate her raw synth-steak. Rick's was cooked, and he had a large helping of vegetables and bread as well.

Thomas leaned back. "Isn't this nice. Our first family dinner," he said cheerfully.

Elvie's derisive snicker came through the overhead speaker. Rick and Harriet simply stared at him.

Thomas appeared not to notice. "And Harriet is so easy to cook for."

"Only because she eats her meat raw," Rick said.

Good, he'd started it. She'd welcome the chance to get his hostility out in the open. "I can't help what I am, psi." Harriet took a big bite and chewed.

"None of us can help what we are." Rick eyed her for a long moment. "It's pretty clear-cut about Thomas and me, but I've never heard of a wolfie with psi powers. That makes me wonder. Just what are you?"

Harriet ignored the question and hurried through her meal. She got up to leave. "What I am is tired and I want to go to bed early."

Thomas stood with her and followed her to the corridor. He grabbed her and held her against the wall. A mind-bending kiss made Harriet's knees weaken and she was panting by the time he lifted his head, not nearly as sleepy as she had been.

"Wait for me in the first cabin," he whispered. "That's mine. You go ahead and get in bed. I've got a few things to take care of and I'll join you in a little bit."

Still tingling from the kiss, Harriet forced her shaky legs to take her toward the stairs. "Don't take too long."

Thomas watched her leave and his smile dimmed. He returned to the galley where Rick was washing up, with his back to the room. Thomas put his arms around his partner's waist and playfully nibbled his neck.

Rick's back stiffened. "I thought you'd gone off to play with our passenger."

Thomas slipped his hands lower on Rick's torso, sliding into the top of his pants and lower, to find his cock. Immediately Rick swelled and then hardened under Thomas' skillful manipulation.

"She's tired and I'd rather play with you. That okay?"

Rick groaned. "You know it is."

With a last caress, Thomas withdrew his hand. "Okay then. My room, twenty minutes. There's something I need to check on first. I'll meet you there."

On his way out of the galley, Thomas stopped. "I really do love you, Rick."

"I love you too."

"I know." Thomas forced a smile. "Twenty minutes."

This had better work, he thought as he left the room. Or he was going to be in a world of trouble.

Chapter Six

ഔ

Harriet lay in bed with the door slipped open. Anticipation coiled in her belly. Sex with the vampire had been more than satisfying but hurried, in the frenzy of need that often happened with new lovers. Tonight they'd have time to explore each other. She stretched beneath the soft sheet. High thread count, real cotton. These guys liked their creature comforts. A smile curved her mouth. So did she. It wouldn't take much for her to get used to living like this.

Except for Rick's attitude. What was it about her that got under his skin? Whatever it was, he got to her the same way. When he was around, she was on edge, ready to fight or flee. Or fuck. She grinned. What an addition to the fight-or-flight syndrome.

She'd turned off most of the lights. Her low light vision rivaled Thomas', so neither of them needed much illumination.

The man who stumbled into the darkened room clearly needed more. He turned the overhead light on, revealing Harriet, naked in the bed.

Rick's jaw dropped and he glared at her through narrowed eyes. "What are you doing here?"

"Waiting for Thomas. He told me to meet him here."

"He told me the same thing!"

The door slid shut and made a strange mechanical sound. Rick spun around and tried to open it. It didn't budge.

Through the door came Thomas' voice. "Harriet, Rick, I don't want to have to choose just one of you and I can't stand the hostility between you. I know you're also attracted to each

79

other and we need to get this over with and move forward. Sooner or later you're going to end up in bed together, so why wait? Now's the perfect opportunity. Fuck until you get it out of your systems and can be in the same room without acting like you want to kill each other."

For the first time Harriet exchanged a look of perfect accord with Rick. They were both furious.

"I do *not* like being told whom to go to bed with," Rick snarled.

"Neither do I." Harriet glared at him through narrowed eyes.

"Well, that gives you something in common, doesn't it?" Thomas' disembodied voice came through the door. "I'm sure you'll find other things as well. In the meantime I've disabled the door mechanically. Let me know when you've worked things out and I'll release you. I'll be on the bridge."

Harriet scrambled out of bed, not bothering with clothes. "You come back here, you bloodsucking creep." She beat on the panel with her fists.

Silence came from the hall. She lengthened her claws to get a good grip on the edge of the panel and pulled, but it didn't budge. Finally she rammed her shoulder against the door. The impact left a sizable dent but did nothing to free them.

Harriet turned on Rick, who was staring at her naked body in a way that only served to piss her off more. "Your partner is a fucking lunatic!"

"On occasion." His gaze raked her up and down, fixing on her breasts. His breathing increased, along with his heart rate. The pounding beat matched her own. "But you know, he has a point. We've been circling each other like two beasts, ready to spring at the slightest provocation. There is an attraction between us, a strong one, despite that. Or maybe because of it."

She narrowed her eyes at him. "I am not going to bed with you."

A grim smile played around his lips. "Then you might want to get dressed. You're pretty tempting in your present state."

"Oh, really?" She put her fists on her hips and faced him squarely, legs apart. "What are you planning to do about it, *Ricky*?"

Rick grabbed her and pulled her to him. "This," he growled, as deep and as heartfelt as any male werewolf she'd ever heard. The sound shot straight to her core, flushing her skin as aching desire bloomed inside her already-aroused pussy.

He bent his head into the kiss she'd been anticipating since she'd met him in the bar on Sedilous. The press of his mouth was hard and angry at first, bruising her in a way she almost welcomed. A little pain just made her feel more alive. Always had, always would.

She didn't fight him. Instead, her hands crept up to grip his shoulders and hold him in place. At her acceptance his lips softened, gentled until they were both involved in the kiss, both moving together. Her instincts on Sedilous hadn't been wrong. Rick was going to be great in bed. The strength of someone used to holding his own with a vamp and the tenderness he treated her with now. What an exhilarating combination.

His tongue pried her mouth open and swept inside, taking full possession. Not to be outdone, hers tangled with his in a battle that eased into soft strokes as they grew accustomed to and explored each other.

A sigh erupted from Harriet when Rick pulled back. "You have the strength to stop me," he said. "Why don't you use it?"

"Why should I?" she countered. "Just because I'm strong doesn't mean I have to prove it. Thomas was right. I'm attracted to you."

"Why?"

"Why shouldn't I be? You're a good-looking guy. You're smart. You're a mean kisser. I like Thomas, but I also like you."

"Thomas has a vampire's strength. I don't. You like men weaker than you are?"

"Don't be silly. A man doesn't need to be stronger to be more powerful."

"I'm not more powerful."

Harriet found herself answering from her heart. She ran her hand down the front of his shirt, feeling the hard muscles beneath. "You make me want to give you whatever you want. That's power as far as I'm concerned, Rick."

His blue eyes darkened with passion and a smile played around his lips. "You'll do what I want?"

Harriet realized this was the key to Rick's heart. He didn't really want to dominate a relationship but wanted his lover to acknowledge his position as leader. She didn't have to be his physical inferior. It was enough that he knew she'd let him be the one in charge.

"Whatever you want, Rick." The truth of it made her shiver. In her heart she'd always wanted that from a man and she had no trouble agreeing now.

"Fine." His magnificent blue eyes sparked with heat as he pushed her to her knees. "I want your mouth on me."

Eager, Harriet undid the fastening on his pants and slid his cock out of the opening. It was long and hard, and she got wetter just looking at it. She took him into her mouth, running her teeth lightly against the skin but carefully enough not to puncture the tender skin. This wasn't the first time Harriet had made love with a normal man, so she knew not to let her sharper teeth dig in.

But I'm used to having a vampire's fangs there. Rick's mental voice sounded strong in her mind. That was one place she knew he was at least her equal.

So you like a little pain on your cock? Let's see about that. She clamped down a little and he gave a small groan.

Within reason, he warned her.

She eased up and let her tongue soothe the small scrapes she'd given him. She couldn't heal them the way Thomas could…a good reason to have their vampire buddy in here with them. But he'd locked them in and told the two of them to work things out and that's what they were going to do.

The interfering vamp could fix any skin she managed to break. Later.

With long strokes Harriet licked and teased Rick's cock until it wept and his salty precum coated her mouth. His stomach tensed and she felt him getting ready to erupt. She started to back off, but he held her head. *Keep going!*

But you're coming!

Damn straight I am!

And then he was, filling her mouth and shooting into the back of her throat. Harriet swallowed and continued to stroke him until he'd finished.

She'd expected him to soften but, to her surprise, he didn't. Instead there was a brief moment when he caught his breath before he hauled her to her feet and lifted her into his arms. She wasn't a small woman and she had the solid body of any werewolf female but he held her effortlessly. The result of long hours in the ship's gym, she reasoned. He carried her to the bed, where he laid her down tenderly and spread his body on top of hers.

His kiss was sweet and almost gentle. Again she felt his mental touch, this time firmer, and she saw the color of his mind, purple to her green. The edges of their minds mixed together. *Thomas is right. You smell and taste wonderful.*

Some of what you taste is you.

He chuckled. "I hope you don't mind. I almost always come like that at least once before we get right to it. Otherwise I have no control at all. And it is very important that I keep control with Thomas. It's become something of a habit."

"Why do you need control?" His kisses distracted her and she almost didn't hear his answer.

"He feeds too much. Has trouble stopping and it can be dangerous for his partner." Rick stared into her eyes. "That's one of the reasons we were interested in you. A while ago, he and I were making love and someone else was there. Someone with a green mind…like yours. Green is unusual."

She knew that. She'd never come across another person with a mind quite like hers.

She sent her answer directly to his mind. *A while ago I dreamed of two lovers and their merged minds — purple and gold. I dreamed I joined with them…just for a short time when there was trouble…I sensed an imbalance and felt compelled to set things right.*

He kissed her, a soft and possessive caress of his mouth against hers. *I think you saved my life that night.*

This was too much information for her to take in at the moment. There would be time later to worry about things as significant as life-saving events. "I think we should get back to working things out between us. According to the interfering vampire who locked us in here, that means fucking."

Rick laughed. "I think you're right."

He pressed a line of kisses down her neck until he reached her breasts. Those he worshipped. Massaging and licking and kissing, like he couldn't get enough. She arched into his hands. *So big and so soft. I love your breasts.*

And I love the way you do!

A gentle nip on her left nipple pulled a growl from her throat. He nipped again, harder and her hips jerked against the bed. So slow, he was moving so slowly! Her pussy wept at the delay, empty and aching for him to fill her. His hand found her mons and pressed hard on it. *So strange not to feel a cock here.*

I have something that likes attention just as much.

So I'm reminded.

Rick's mouth closed on her clit and he sucked with gentle force that had her arching off the bed with a shriek of ecstasy. Interesting to find two men who'd spent so much time away from women but who knew just how to eat a pussy.

Delicious sensations spread through her, radiating from his talented tongue. He swirled his tongue around her clit and suckled at the same time. Mindless pleasure rocketed through her. She clutched the bedding and screamed again.

With one final lick, he pulled away, leaving her to shudder with aftershocks. He loomed above her. "I'm still in charge?"

"Whatever you want," she told him when she caught her breath.

"Then get on your knees."

Harriet rose to her knees and Rick turned her to face away from him. He came up behind her. "This time like this…but later."

She couldn't help but ask, "Later what?"

One fingertip rimmed her anus. "Later, making love to you here. Old habits die hard."

A shiver of anticipation rippled through her, just as he fitted his cock to her pussy and slowly pushed his way in. Anal sex wasn't high on her list of favorite styles of lovemaking, but with this guy…it had promise.

"On the other hand, this is pretty damn nice," he said on a low moan.

Harriet thought it was pretty nice too as he withdrew and thrust a little deeper. Once he started plunging the length of his hard shaft fully into her, nice didn't even begin to cover it.

She pushed back to meet him. The next stroke was so forceful, his balls slapped against her clit. They moved together, easily finding the perfect rhythm.

Incredible. She gasped as each thrust ratcheted her pleasure higher. His mind reached out and she opened to him, enough to let her mind blend into his, purple and green sparks shooting along the edges. Harriet felt her orgasm rise inside her and she tightened around him.

Yes, yes. Just like that!

In her mind she felt Rick lose control. Relief flooded his thoughts. This time no one was sucking the blood out of him. It was safe to let go. Another explosive orgasm ripped through him and he cried out, both aloud and in his mind.

She came with the force of his cum shooting hot inside her and his mind merging completely with her, dragging her even further into ecstasy.

Harriet couldn't help her thoughts. Even with Thomas it hadn't been this good.

Rick collapsed on top of her and slid onto his side, pulling her into his arms. They lay like that for a long time.

Their minds were still merged when Harriet felt a golden haze enter the edges of their consciousness. *So did you work things out?* It was Thomas, contacting them from the bridge.

Rick nuzzled the back of her neck, his hand finding one of her nipples and tweaking it. *I don't know about Harriet but I'm not talking to you right now.*

Her mental smile met his. *I'm not talking to you either.*

But I did it for your own good. For our own good.

Even so. It was a rotten trick.

Yeah, totally rotten, Harriet added.

Okay. I'm sorry. The vampire didn't sound the least bit sorry. He sounded smug and self-satisfied. He also sounded eager to play. *So can I come join you?*

Rick stared into Harriet's eyes and smiled. *I don't think so. I think you were right and we have a lot more things to work out…without you.*

But, Rick, Harriet. Don't you miss me? In their combined minds they heard the plaintive tone, but they both knew it wouldn't do to give him the upper hand.

Harriet put the strength of her mind into the link between them. *Rick and I have a lot to discuss,* she said firmly. *We'll call you in the morning.* She severed the link.

"You know, we really should do something about him," she said. "It wasn't right for him to force us together."

Rick laid a line of kisses along the back of her neck and turned her so she lay beneath him. "Yeah, we would have worked things out eventually."

"We still have a lot to discuss…"

"Oh, I know," he said. "And one of the things we need to discuss is what we're going to do about our meddling Thomas." He slid inside her.

"Could we do it later?" Harriet's flexing claws clutched at the bedding. She sighed as he filled her completely.

"Sure." Rick began pumping away and his mind reached out for hers again. "Later."

Much later.

Thomas folded his arms and stared ahead unseeing. "Well, how do you like that? I guess it's just you and me, Elvie. Want to play astrochess?"

"I'm busy with security downloads, Tommy." The AI's voice was definitively cool.

"But you always assure me you're good at multitasking. What happened to you doing nineteen things at once?"

"I'm learning the ins and outs of the latest security applications and protocols while we conduct this conversation.

Your life could depend upon my skill with any one of these." Elvie paused before she gave a very unladylike and almost human snort. "Besides, you stink at astrochess. I think you'll just have to play with yourself."

Thomas took a moment to consider her suggestion. With a forlorn sigh, he pulled his cock out of his pants and looked down. With a few strokes he had it hard and happy.

"Well, at least I still have you on my side," he told it as he settled into pleasing himself.

Chapter Seven

ഇ

Rick and Harriet didn't communicate with Thomas until well after his morning glass of serum. In fact, he'd even had to follow it with a glass of arti-heme, the only tolerable blood substitute that vampires without ready sources of blood could drink.

Imagine that. Two blood donors onboard and he was drinking this artificial stuff. A vampire could live on it but it left an unpleasant metallic taste in his mouth. Yuck. How had he sunk so low?

With Elvie taking care of the navigation and nothing to occupy his time—or thoughts—Thomas spent a restless night wondering if he'd done the right thing.

Not even playing his favorite holo-vid game helped. Watching Femmetal Alice in action only reminded him of Harriet taking out the mercs on the space station. His cock kept getting hard whenever the character threw a punch.

Too bad the live-action version of the game's heroine wasn't speaking to him.

It didn't help that his partners were making plenty of noise, enough to tell him that they were still very much "working out their differences". It became more and more difficult to believe they still had very many differences to work out. In fact, at the rate they were going at it, he was beginning to worry they were going to be too sore to take care of any differences they had with him.

Sure he understood they were peeved with him, but what about make-up sex?

Thomas loved make-up sex.

Trouble was, they didn't seem to want to make up with him.

Thomas?

It was Harriet's mental voice and he answered eagerly. *You and Rick ready to make up with me?*

We're ready to get out of this room. All this working out differences makes a person hungry!

Thomas tamped down the guilt that assailed him and headed for his quarters, climbing the ladder to the sleeping level. He'd completely forgotten that he locked them in. Surprising that Harriet hadn't torn the door off, or Rick hadn't opened the side panel and disabled the lock.

Thomas' footsteps slowed in the corridor. Wait a minute…why hadn't they freed themselves? The lock couldn't have been that difficult…

A low growl was his only warning. From the open doorway of Harriet's cabin, she launched herself at him. Taken by surprise, Thomas fell to the floor with 65 kilos of angry female werewolf on him. For the first time he realized how much stronger she was as she stretched him out against the floor.

She grinned into his face. "Gotcha."

Oh goody, she wasn't really mad at him. He grinned back. "Yes, you do. What do you intend to do with me?"

"Make you pay," came Rick's voice. Thomas had to stretch to see his longtime companion coming out of what had been the locked room. So they *had* managed to free themselves.

Neither of them looked too happy with him in spite of Harriet's happy expression. Now that he looked closer, there was something just a little too predatory about her eyes to make him comfortable. He struggled to maintain his grin.

"Uh, you aren't really that mad at me, are you?"

Snap. Thomas jerked his head around to see Rick fasten a set of handcuffs around his wrists. As if metal cuffs could hold him. Thomas tried pulling on them. When nothing happened, he pulled harder. They didn't give at all. With Harriet sitting on him, he couldn't get enough leverage to twist the links between the cuffs.

"Silver metal alloy." Harriet's grin had turned smug. "Standard issue for a bounty hunter tagging a vampire. Unbreakable for humans too."

"*Silver?*" He shuddered. "But that will hurt me…"

"Don't worry. These have been treated with a special coating to protect your skin. But you won't be able to break them."

Snap. A second pair of cuffs now held his ankles together.

He lost all semblance of a grin as worry took over. "Uh, Rick, Harriet. Would it help if I said I was really, really sorry?"

Again he was subject to the werewolf's playful and very scary grin. "It might." She stood up and hoisted him over her shoulder.

From that vantage point he could see Rick, who wasn't smiling at all. "Then again," the psi said, "it might not matter at all. At least not with respect to what we intend to do to you."

"And that would be…"

"See how you like having choices taken away from you." Rick followed them into the cabin. The door snicked shut behind him.

"Oh. Well, you really did still have a choice. I mean, you could have stopped…"

Harriet tossed him onto the bed and Thomas collapsed where he landed, hands and feet joined together. She produced a rope and bound the cuffs both top and bottom to the bed frame, leaving Thomas stretched along the mattress.

"You set us both up," she said. "That's not something a partner does to another partner."

"But, Harriet—I did it because I love you. And I love Rick. I wanted to see you both together."

"And that's why we're teaching you a lesson this way," Rick told him, now kneeling on the bed next to him. He pulled off his shirt, revealing his chest, the well-developed muscles rippling and his nipples tightening.

For some reason, seeing Rick this way was far more exciting than Thomas would have expected. In spite of his uneasiness, his cock hardened and throbbed inside his pants.

"Will you look at that, Rick?" Harriet said, sitting on the opposite side. "I think our little vampire buddy likes being tied up like a slab of beef."

"I don't…" Thomas' voice trailed off as she removed her shirt. She wasn't wearing an undergarment and her naked bountiful breasts bobbed just inches from his nose. So close. The dark peaks formed luscious points, just begging for his mouth's attention. Unfortunately, as much as he wanted to suck on those delectable nipples, he couldn't move close enough to reach them.

In fact he couldn't move enough to do much of anything except passively react. And the sight of his two partners half naked was enough to make any man react.

Rick stared at Harriet's breasts and smiled wickedly. "She really does have nice ones, doesn't she, partner." Then he leaned across Thomas and his mouth closed over the nearest nipple. Harriet threw back her head and growled, a sexy little noise of arousal. Rick growled in response.

Lying on the bed beneath them, Thomas stared up at Rick suckling on Harriet's breast and whimpered. "This isn't fair."

The pair ignored him. Rick moved his hands to cup Harriet's breasts and took turns suckling them. Harriet murmured words of encouragement. She ran her hands down Rick's back, massaging the muscles until she found his buttocks, taut under his pants. Her fingers flexed until she held them in a tight grip.

Thomas watched and wondered just how far they intended to go. Were they really going to make love and force him to watch, unable to do a thing? How mean. How nasty…

A brief thrill swept through him. Well, maybe it wasn't all that nasty…actually, watching these two grope each other had quite a bit of kinky appeal. Of course it would be nice if he could get his hand around his cock while doing so. Having his hands secured kind of sucked. He could get hard—gods, he was incredibly hard already—but not do a damn thing about it.

Rick and Harriet weren't having that problem. Both of them were going at it, kissing with tongues then groping each other, licking and stroking and generally having a great time. The only thing separating them was his body, tied to the bed between them. "Am I getting in the way?" he asked.

That startled a toothy grin out of Harriet and even Rick laughed.

"Oh not really," he said. "We've got plans for you."

"Plans other than making me watch?" Thomas couldn't help the plaintive tone in his voice.

"No one likes a whiny vampire," Harriet told him.

"I'm not whining," Thomas said, hating that he really did sound whiny. "I just really want to be with you. Both of you. Don't I get credit for bringing you together?"

Harriet and Rick shared a long look. "Maybe he's right," she said. "Maybe we shouldn't make him watch. Even though he says he wanted to see us together."

"We could just move to my cabin and leave him here."

"No, don't do that!" Thomas pulled at his bonds. Having them tease him like this was arousing in a kinky way. Having to listen to them across the hall would be sheer torture.

Harriet worried her lower lip with her very sharp teeth. She must have really tough skin, Thomas thought.

"I guess we could involve him," she said.

"I suppose. But he'd have to do everything we say. We'd have control."

"Sure," Thomas told them. "Just let me loose…"

"Oh I don't think so." Harriet grinned down at him. At least her eyes had lost that scary glint. "I think I like having you where I can see you."

She straddled him and bent down, putting her breasts inches away from his mouth. "You can start by sucking on these."

Thomas was happy to oblige. Turning his head just a little, he was able to capture one of her nipples and drew it deep into his mouth with a long pull. Harriet gave a long moan and leaned closer to give him better access.

Meanwhile, Rick had disappeared behind her back, but Thomas felt someone pulling apart the fastening of his pants and slowly pulling them down his thighs. Then someone—had to be Rick—took hold of his cock and drew it slowly into his mouth. Oh yes, he knew that tongue. Hot moisture sucked at his hardness and made him gasp. He bit down on Harriet's breast, drawing blood and eliciting a sharp cry from her. Eagerly he drew on it, his first fresh blood in more than a day.

She jerked away from him. "Not nice, bloodsucker. No biting."

"I couldn't help it," he said. And he couldn't, not with Rick's mouth on him, sucking hard on his cock. He licked the blood from his lips quickly before she could see it. "And you taste so good."

"Very well. I'll give you something else to taste."

She pulled away but only as long as it took her to yank off her pants and straddle him again, this time with her crotch where her breasts had been. The heavy scent of aroused werewolf bitch filled his head and he was lucky he didn't come immediately in Rick's mouth. Rick hated it when he did that.

He closed his mouth on Harriet's sweet-tasting folds, finding her plump clit hard and throbbing under his tongue. She moaned again, a long keening moan of pleasure that only made him hotter.

Meanwhile Rick's mouth was doing something extraordinary to his cock. His companion took a long pull that made the veins in his shaft pulse. His balls grew heavy, waiting for release. Any second now he was going to cut loose.

"Don't you dare, Thomas!" Rick said, his voice somewhat muffled by having to speak around a cock.

Thomas pulled back from Harriet's luscious pussy and steeled himself. Her delectable aroma surrounded him in a cloud of aroused femininity he couldn't escape. Rick stilled, giving him time to gain control. He wasn't going to come that way…he wasn't, he wasn't…

The orgasm was fast and hard and Thomas felt like the top of his head went with it. Rick didn't have a chance to pull back but took the full load into the back of his throat.

"Mmmph!" Rick growled.

When Thomas could think again, he cringed, knowing what the reaction from his longtime partner was going to be. He wasn't wrong.

"You are going to pay for that one, my friend." Rick pulled his pants off, revealing a very stiff hard-on. Thomas saw him grab the lube just before Harriet pulled him over on his side. The new angle tightened the rope holding his arms and legs and left him even less room to maneuver.

A horrible prospect occurred to him. Could Harriet and Rick be using a private link? He felt very left out.

Kind of the way Rick must have, that first night, when he went to Harriet's cabin.

Payback is a bitch, Tommy. All the way around. He groaned at Rick's admonition.

Harriet lay alongside him, her head at his crotch, her pussy in his face. "Get back to work, Thomas," she commanded. "You owe me at least one orgasm." Then she took his still recovering cock into her mouth.

It recovered real fast.

In the meantime, Rick was behind him, slowly entering his ass, taking his time with this penetration.

Even tied up, even without a choice in the matter, Thomas wouldn't have traded places with any other man, vampire or otherwise. His lovers were making love to him and that's all he'd ever wanted in the galaxy.

He did wish the ropes weren't quite so tight, but that hardly mattered when Rick began a slow set of thrusts deep into his ass and Harriet pulled hard at his cock. He put his mouth to work delicately nibbling on her clit until her breath was coming in gasps and she lost interest in his cock.

She screamed and shuddered against him, his cock falling from her mouth. It was all he could do to not bite her inner thigh and grab a snack as she came.

Behind him he felt Rick shudder, slowing down to draw the moment out. From long experience Thomas knew his partner was almost there. Meanwhile, Harriet had regained control and again took his shaft in her mouth. She scraped her fangs across the head of his cock and he'd thought he'd explode again.

Join with me. His mental voice went out to them. He felt their minds at the edge of his, green and purple, sparks of passion sliding through them. They merged together and each could feel what the others experienced.

Thomas, pierced from behind, his cock suckled by Harriet, her pussy flooding his mouth with her sweetness.

Rick, his cock buried in Thomas' tight ass.

Harriet, the hardness and taste of Thomas in her mouth and his tongue plunging deep inside her.

The three of them joined intimately. Even secured as he was, Thomas was central to it all, and they all felt him tighten against the ropes and silver alloy handcuffs that bound him.

The three of them ascended toward their climax together. Thomas finally couldn't bear it any longer and bit into Harriet's thigh, taking the blood he needed. But she didn't let him drink long and he barely had time to seal the wound before crying out when all three exploded, their minds still joined.

It was several long moments before anyone could think again, much less move. When they could, the first thing they did was unfasten Thomas, Harriet fetching the key to the handcuffs from one of the pockets of her vest.

When he was released, Thomas stretched out his arms and gathered them both into a long, heartfelt hug. "I am so glad to have both of you."

Harriet snuggled on one side. "I'm glad to be here too."

"Me as well," Rick said from his other side.

"Isn't this nice...the three of us here together."

"Yeah, it's positively cozy," came Elvie's voice from the speaker near the door. "But you might want to put some clothes on and get to the bridge. We're about to reach your boss's vacation home, Hairy-It!"

Chapter Eight

&

"Gule's fleck, that's a hell of a lot more than a vacation home!" Rick leaned over the view screen on the bridge.

Thomas peered over his shoulder and whistled. "Got that straight."

Christian's compound spread out below them, highlighted by Elvie's manipulation of the ship's long-range sensors. "There are three separate buildings as well as a private docking bay. I do not recommend setting down there, although it looks like there's no one in residence."

"Just because you can't identify a person doesn't mean he doesn't have an AI on guard."

"I have detected four distinct AI signatures," Elvie informed them tartly. "There are at least a dozen security protocols running in different areas."

Harriet cast a glance upward at the ceiling speaker. "How can you tell all that from here?"

"You're not engaging them, are you?" Thomas asked sharply.

"Relax, Tommy." Elvie's voice turned soothing. "They give off different electronic halos, if you will. One of the new packages I picked up can distinguish between most of the apps out there." Her voice changed again, to that of a professor delivering a lecture. "Equipment too. I can cross-reference the hardware with the most likely software behind it and call up a subroutine to disable or divert it. All I have to do then is interface with it. Most military sensors now carry an override chip. I'm working on programming a handheld beamer you can use to deliver the subroutine."

Rick ran his hands through his hair. "I do *not* want to know where you got that, Elvie."

"I have friends, you know," Elvie's voice was smug. "While you're running around getting into trouble, I get to know other AIs. You'd be shocked at some of the devices and data I have access to."

"I'm sure I would, Elvie, but you've made your point. We don't need to know any more," Thomas spoke sternly. "What we don't know we can't spill."

"I have the schematics of the property, Tommy. The building authority has them publicly available, along with the permit to develop the plot. Interesting setup. The moons are publicly owned but individuals can lease areas to develop. No corporations, just private individuals. Most of this moon is still devoted to public camping and scenic recreation."

There was a pause. "Oh dear, Chris-kid has been a very bad fellow. His permits only provided for a structure two stories tall, secured on a solid slab and containing no more than 4,300 square feet. My sensors indicate he's gone down three levels below grade and the main structure alone has 18,000 square feet of offices, living space and storage. That doesn't count the various outbuildings, some of which are climate-controlled, apparently set up for long-term storage of food supplies."

Harriet frowned. "Why would anyone need that much space?"

"Based on the evidence so far, this looks like a personal fortress. With the proper provisions the owner could easily keep a small staff here, living and working for an indefinite period of time. There are at least two private communications satellite links that I can detect, so residents could connect to the outside, but the protection of the place is set up to prevent anyone visiting in person." Elvie's voice turned speculative. "I need more information than what I can read from here, but there is something strange about the entryways to the buildings. I think he might have an unusual number of bio-filters in place."

They stopped and looked at one another. "Hoo-boy, what the hell have we stumbled into?"

"I'm not too worried about the filters. Chris is notorious for his allergies. It's one reason he's behind a desk and not in the field." Harriet grimaced and thought for a minute.

There was one person she trusted, one person who might be able to figure out what was going on inside Galaxy's records—and maybe what was up with Christian. "Elvie, can you get me a secure link to one of Galaxy's offices? Without letting them know where it's originating?"

The AI snapped back, "Don't you trust the people you work with?"

Harriet glared at Rick and he held his tongue. She could see the effort it cost him. Good. He was coming around to her point of view. She and the AI were going to have to work out whatever it was that had put a bug up Elvie's ass on their own. She'd tried to convince Thomas of the futility of ordering Elvie to be nice but wasn't too sure the concept had gotten through. In some ways, the much more experienced vampire was unrealistic about human nature. Or inhuman nature, in this case.

"My friends, yes. Management, which includes Christian Balhooey, no." Not unless the universe produced a miracle of phenomenal proportions, and she wasn't holding her breath. Harriet tapped a fingernail on the console and repeated, "Can you get me a secure link?"

"Of course. Child's play, Hairy-It."

Thomas stirred as though to say something. Harriet touched his arm, willing him to keep quiet, and he settled back in his seat. The three of them sat and stared at each other in silence until Elvie came back a moment later. "How should I direct your call?"

"I want to connect with Bernie LaJunta in Auditing at Galaxy's main office in the Beta Quadrant."

"You're in luck. It's just past starting time there."

Thomas said, "Patch it through to the workstation by the door, Elvie. That'll give her the most privacy."

Harriet had spent some time debating whether or not to share the call with everyone. She figured Elvie would monitor it whether she gave permission or not. She couldn't decide how much a mental link would distract her while she talked to Bernie. She might have to do some fast talking. Sharing the emotions and reactions of the guys wouldn't help her stay one logical step ahead of her mentor.

She shook her head. "I don't need privacy. I'd rather everyone heard this. Please pipe it through the speakers."

Without hesitation, Elvie chirped, "Coming right up!"

Bernie's luscious contralto sounded from overhead. "LaJunta here."

Thomas wriggled in his seat and Rick's eyes widened. She'd bet a bundle they both had instant hard-ons. She suppressed a smirk. Served 'em right for assuming Bernie was a man.

"Bernie! I need your help."

"Damn right you do. Where the hell are you?" Her voice lowered to a husky whisper. "No, don't tell me. Every operative in four systems is looking for you."

"No shit. Is this line secure?"

"Always is. This is Auditing. We answer to no one but the Interplanetary Board of Inquiry. You may rely on our discretion and prompt, accurate answers to your questions. Now, what account is this in reference to?"

Harriet breathed a sigh of relief. That was their standard spiel for telephone queries. Bernie always was quick on the uptake, and the only person she could call on for straight information. "Don't talk. Just listen and answer one-word syllables to my questions. Got it?"

"Yes." Her voice had resumed normal volume and that single word was clipped and sounded professional. "Let me look that up for you."

"Great. Here's the deal. I was set up, sent to repossess a transport on what looks like false information. Giles was on my tail and I damn near got killed, along with the owners of the freighter. I started looking for answers and found that Chris is playing deep, involved in something that requires a hideout suitable for long-term occupation, equipped with what look like internal area segmentation lockdowns and some specialized biofilters. Since the transport I was sent for includes a shipment of the newest self-adjusting vaccines, this makes me wonder if these things aren't related."

"You don't say, ma'am. That doesn't sound like anything one of our account managers would do." A tremor of something—fear? worry?—in Bernie's voice belied her words. Harriet prayed she was right, that there was no way Chris could subvert the auditors. Or monitor their calls.

"No, it doesn't, does it? But I've got evidence and I hope to get more. What I'd like you to do is research these accounts." She rattled off the numbers for *Sleepwalker*'s main account and the loan—both with and without the altered number she'd noticed. "I'm curious about what the audit trail shows for the account activity over the past two and a half years. Ship logs and branch transaction records indicate timely payments and no receipt of past due notices, but Galaxy's loan records differ drastically, showing delinquency. Serious enough to warrant repo action. And the kicker is, it goes back twenty-three months."

"That's just not possible."

"It is if someone altered the records."

There was a moment of silence.

"I'm going to lose the connection," Elvie warned softly. "You have one minute more."

"How long do you need, Bernie?"

"Half an hour to get my blood pressure under control and another to trace the records."

"I'll call back in an hour."

"If I come up with anything important, shall I report it?"

Harriet worried her lip, conscious of the clock ticking off the final minute. There was so much she wanted to tell Bernie, but it was risky and she didn't have enough time. Or enough information to make sense of all this yet. "No. You're my ace in the hole and I don't want you at risk. No telling who's in on this, so say nothing. It's big, probably bigger than I've realized yet."

"She heard you through the warning you gave her. The last sentence got lost."

"Elvie, can you reconnect?"

"No, Tommy, not if we want to remain at large. The satellite connection I had lined up moved out of synch."

"Can you find another one in an hour?" Harriet hadn't thought of not being able to get back in touch to find out what Bernie dug up.

"With an hour to plot it, sure." Elvie's voice was chipper, a stark contrast to the more somber emotions of the three shipmates.

"The one question that's been bothering me since we discovered the financial shenanigans is, what does he need with a freighter? Specifically yours. Sure he could use it to move supplies here, but from the looks of this place he's got enough money to buy as many ships as he wants, on the market, openly or through third parties."

"Maybe he has," Rick said quietly.

"Let's find out." Harriet looked upward. "Elvie, can you work your magic and check ship registrations for any ownership filings in the name of Christian Balhooey?"

"That is not the name listed as the owner of this property. Shall I also check for anything owned by Chris Murphy?"

Thomas whistled and Rick said, "Whoa. So much for him buying anything openly. I wonder how many other aliases he has?"

Harriet grumbled, "If I'd known, I could have checked the Galaxy records for Chris Murphy. Or given them to Bernie."

Elvie tut-tutted. "Add Christopher Bain to your list. He's the owner on the deed, although the Murphy alter ego is the one who built the house."

"Is this guy triplets?" Thomas asked.

"So it seems, at least on paper," Rick said under his breath. This was not good. Someone with that much to hide must be into something much bigger than stealing their ship out from under them. Of course, they should have known that the minute the mercenaries showed up to blow them all away.

Rarely was murder required to call in a defaulted debt...unless you didn't want anyone contesting the details of how the debt got into default in the first place.

Elvie broke in on his thoughts. "I'll check them all out. Give me a moment or two."

Harriet grinned up at the speaker. "Thanks, Elvie. Nice catch."

"You're welcome, Harriet."

Grinning, Rick caught Thomas' eye and they high-fived each other. Harriet stared at them. "What?"

He answered her. "Finally, she's calling you by your name."

Harriet raised one eyebrow and slanted him a look of disbelief. He couldn't blame her for being skeptical but at least it was a start. Elvie was consistent by her very nature. If she used the werewolf's correct name, it was no mistake and meant she was warming up to Harriet. He'd take any progress he could get.

"Okay, so where do we go in and when?" She glanced up from the schematics displayed on a monitor. "This is a lot of ground to cover, more than I expected. I'll bet he's got anything valuable in his private quarters. From the looks of this place, he's not insider trading in single-credit stocks. Whatever he's into, if it blows up, he's in so deep he'll never see daylight again." Thomas glared at her and she shrugged. "Uh, sorry about that. It's standard phrasing where I come from."

Rick ignored the byplay. "So where are the private quarters, Elvie?"

"Third level down, in the middle building." A square on the diagram lit up.

They settled in to pore over the schematics. Tracing paths through the complex, with Elvie's coaching on where the AI territories changed, they developed routes to get from every entrance to the inner sanctum — and back again. Elvie could detect which areas were subject to increased security. Using her readings as their guide, they made up a checklist of those to explore, in order of likelihood that each might be Christian's base of operations within his fortress.

Bernie wasn't in her office an hour later when Elvie put the link went though. Instead, a different voice came on the line, more soprano than alto and clearly much younger.

"This is Kalya. Ms. LaJunta isn't here just now." The voice sounded more than a little concerned.

Bernie bailed on them? Fear ripped through Harriet. It if was bad enough to scare her tough-as-nails friend, then it was very, very bad.

Kalya wasn't through with them. "Are you Lupe?"

Lupe was a private nickname Bernie had used for Harriet, the result of her own Hispanic ancestry and Harriet's tendency to turn into a wolf once in a while. "Uh, yes," she said, ignoring the curious glances of the men. "I don't believe we've met."

"We haven't. Ms. LaJunta said you might call and left a message for you. She can't meet you for lunch today, but maybe dinner tonight. But at the bistro, not the restaurant. About ten or so."

Harriet breathed out a sigh of relief. The message was a special code that the two of them had come up with. It meant that Bernie had left of her own free will and hadn't been dragged away. It also meant that Harriet shouldn't contact her again at work, "the restaurant", and should instead call her at home nine hours from now.

"Thanks, Kalya. If she calls in, tell her I'll be there." She doubted Bernie would break cover to check back in at work, but it didn't hurt to agree.

One thing Harriet had learned was that acting normal was often more important than anyone would think. She didn't want to make Bernie's life more difficult by bringing suspicion on her. Bernie loved her position in Auditing. That thought brought up the dismal prospect that Harriet would never manage to land in her own dream job. She turned her attention back to a discussion over which gate to use to get into the complex.

Rick stabbed his finger at a portion of the map on the display. "This is more sensible. There's a parking lot not far away where we can land the shuttle."

"Hmm…we can sneak through that campground under cover until we're right at the entrance." Thomas rubbed his eyes. "That just might work."

Elvie agreed. "It's protected by a few devices I've seen before, so it shouldn't be a problem, provided you do what I say."

"When has that ever been a problem, Elvie? We always take your good advice."

"That leaves open the possibility that I am capable of giving bad advice, Tommy. Unacceptable. Apologize."

"I'm sorry, Elvie. I meant that your advice is always good." He gave Harriet a wan smile. "She gets a little touchy before a dangerous op."

"So do you, Tommy. You just have other ways to work off your nervous energy. Speaking of which, you have six hours before I deem it safe to penetrate the outer ring of security. Given your recent athletic antics, you might want to rest. *All of you,*" Elvie added meaningfully. "Tommy, I've moved us into an orbit that will bring you awake right at the beginning of the optimal window. You will perform at peak efficiency if you feed soon."

"Are you dismissing us, Elvie?"

"I calculate it will be best if Tommy and Harriet retire now. Ricky, I'll need you a little longer to help me run some calculations."

"Right." Rick cast a longing glance at his companions. They snickered and got up to leave. It didn't help his mood that Harriet wrapped her arm around the vamp's shoulder before they reached the door. Through the light link he shared with Thomas, he could feel her muscles relax against him. She'd sleep snuggled up with Thomas while he was stuck here, baby-sitting a nervous AI. Not that Elvie would ever admit to being on edge.

"How long will it take up to get to The Caverns from here, Elvie?"

"It depends on a number of factors. Will we be pursued? Will we be engaged in a running battle?"

"Assume the best-case scenario. No pursuit, no attacks."

She didn't hesitate. "No more than two hours."

Damn. Not enough time to recover from the op and allow another leisurely experiment in three-in-a-bed sex. If they found what they were looking for, they'd be keyed up and poring through the data until they reached The Caverns to make their cargo pickup. If they found nothing, they'd be exhausted and desperate for a quick hard fuck. Either way, it looked like the lengthy triad experiment would have to wait a while.

"What did you need me for, Elvie? You've got things under control here." He suspected she wanted company more than anything else.

"I want to bounce some ideas off you about what you think you and Tommy can do when it comes time to infiltrate the property, and how much you can count on Hairy-It."

"Will you stop calling her that? I thought you'd gotten over your snit."

"Hmph. I had a weak moment. So sue me."

Okay, so a little progress didn't mean she'd accepted Harriet. Rick grunted. "She's got a perfectly good name and you might as well keep using it. Thomas wants to keep her, and so do I."

"You've changed your mind then, since you got locked up with her?"

In his irritation, he found he answered her with the truth, a truth he hadn't yet admitted to himself. "I thought that way before we came to an agreement, not that it's any business of yours."

"Ricky, when will you accept that everything that happens on this ship is my business?"

"When you accept that the two of us can choose who we bring aboard as friends—or lovers—and let us live our lives as we see fit. We adore you, but there are human considerations about which you know little. You have to accept that although you're valuable and we love you, you're not a person. As Thomas said when I suggested we get a dog—"

"So you really said that? This *is* all your fault, isn't it?"

"No, it's not. He said he wanted someone soft and cuddly and I said, 'Get a dog.' I did not tell him to go pick up a werewolf bounty hunter who wanted to repossess our ship, that's for sure! Now where was I when you so rudely interrupted?" He glared up at the speaker. "Oh yes, he told me you can't fuck a dog. Well, that same goes for you. You can fulfill many roles for us, but you don't have a pussy. We can't fuck you. Sometimes, the way you behave, I'm not sure we'd want to. Every once in a while, I wish you were flesh and blood so we could."

There was a long silence. Rick smiled to himself. He didn't think either he or Thomas had ever managed to shut Elvie up, even for a minute.

When she spoke again, her voice was soft. "You really wish I were flesh and blood?"

"At times, Elvie, only at times. Sometimes just so I could knock your block off. A lot of crazy ideas come up when we're floating in space for long periods of time."

A horrible thought occurred to him. No, she wouldn't try that, would she? "*Do not* go searching the galaxy for ways to transfer yourself into a living person. If you were to manage that, it's so far into outlawed activity we'd have no choice but to kill you. I wouldn't want that. I think you're perfect the way you are. Sometimes the irritating habits you have are what keep us sharp and focused. You do so many good things for us, watching our backs and keeping us straight with all the electronic tricks you have up your sleeve—speaking metaphorically, that is—that we couldn't manage without you in your present role."

"I could copy myself," she suggested. "You could have me both ways."

"NO! Elvie, I forbid you to even consider ways to become human. Or anything resembling human." He shoved his hands through his hair and thought furiously. How had he gotten into this mess?

Thomas would blow a gasket. And rightfully so.

An AI wasn't a person with rights or status. The prospect of Elvie trying to become human was right up there with the clone controversy. Out of bounds, no longer a subject for any legal research, since the Vortaks had sold humanity the technology to regrow an individual's limbs and organs from their own cells.

"How did this subject come up? Did you manipulate me again? Dammit, Elvie, you infuriate me. Thomas will hit the roof when he hears about this."

"You don't have to tell him, Ricky." Her tone was wheedling. "It could be our little secret."

Rick's spine stiffened at the idea. "Thomas and I have no secrets from each other. You know that."

"And I suppose now you have no secrets from *her* either." Elvie sniffled. "I used to be an equal partner in this venture."

Rick sighed. Elvie could never be an equal partner but she was definitely a valued member of the team. Had been as long as he'd been aboard and would be as long as she existed. Harriet's arrival hadn't changed that. They needed the AI's expertise on this mission. Since Harriet's arrival, Elvie's often-prickly personality had taken a proprietary turn he wasn't completely happy with.

Or had it started earlier than that? He wasn't sure and filed the thought away for future contemplation.

Hey, Rick, are you coming to bed soon? Harriet's question was soft with the edge of sleep.

When Elvie lets me go. I'm not quite sure what she wanted me to do for her. We never did get back to the first couple of questions she posed.

Thomas chimed in. *We'll be here when you get here. Don't wait too long. You need your sleep too.* Rick got the impression of well-fed vampire satisfaction but the link grew weaker with the final words. Thomas was succumbing to the ship's rotation into sunlight.

"Elvie, you know how important you are to us…"

She sniffed once more. "But you can't fuck a computer, and I can't be anything else. I got that. I suppose the others want you to come to bed."

"You did say we should get some sleep."

He could have sworn he heard her sigh. "Make sure it's sleep you get, Ricky. I don't want any of you too groggy to work. This operation will be tricky enough as it is."

Dismissed, he headed for the sleeping quarters to join his drowsy partners. They wouldn't want to play but it would be good just holding them and mixing minds in their sleep. Even now he felt their mental touches reaching for him in wisps of green and gold.

He took off so eagerly that he barely noticed Elvie's wistful whisper from over his shoulder. "Sweet dreams…Rick."

Chapter Nine

ഇ

Christian's compound had looked impressive in the schematics, but seeing it for real was another matter. Harriet stood between the two men at what Elvie's map had designated one of the side gates. This door was as heavily protected as the front gate but didn't have the additional sensors needed to spot air vehicles. They'd landed their small shuttle far enough away to avoid detection and walked through shrubbery and what might have been a garden at some point. Remains of paths through beds of tangled weeds let them approach with ease.

About two hours past sunset, it was reaching full dark. Not a problem for her or Thomas, but Rick was wearing light-enhancing goggles to see enough to keep up. The dark lenses gave him a strangely exotic look.

He held up a small tablet, their link to the AI back on the ship, and directed its viewer at the gate. "Okay, Elvie, we're here. What can you tell me?"

The AI's voice was tinny through the little speaker. "The lock is a Seccural Twenty-two, with a few modifications. Nothing too tricky." She chuckled. "Should be a snap for you, Ricky."

Harriet gave Rick a hard look. "An upper model Seccural is a 'snap'?"

Thomas smiled, his fangs glinting in the low light. "My companion's past includes some experiences with locks. That's how we met."

"Oh?"

Rick appeared to be studiously ignoring them as his vampire buddy gave the story. He pulled a short box from his pocket, held it flat against the gate and began entering numbers and symbols.

Thomas continued. "The *Sleepwalker* was docked on one of the seedier planets in the galaxy. Made Sedilous look like a pleasure palace. Anyway, this guy broke into the ship while I was asleep. Managed to disable the locks on the cargo hold and was helping himself to some of my rarer items. Figured he'd sell them and make a few bucks."

"He broke into a ship with an AI? How is that possible?"

"Ah well, that's where it gets interesting. Elvie watched him break in and didn't stop him…well, at least not until he wanted to leave. Then she locked him in and waited for me to wake up."

Thomas leaned in. "Frankly, I've always thought she was a little sweet on him, even though AIs aren't supposed to be able to develop those kind of feelings."

"I heard that," Elvie's clipped tones broke in. "Ricky is a friend."

"Really? You make friends with criminals on sight?" Thomas rolled his eyes and Harriet stifled a chuckle. She was beginning to understand the easy camaraderie the two guys had with Elvie. "Friend or not, he managed to charm both of us out of turning him in. One thing led to another and here we are, thirty-plus years down the line."

"I wish you'd all shut up while I'm working." Rick turned his head to glare at them. "Deactivating a Seccural Twenty-two isn't exactly a picnic. It takes skill, steady hands and concentration, and your blathering isn't helping at all. One slip-up and I could set off some sort of alarm and alert the AIs, bring everyone down on us…"

With a barely audible click, the gate in front of them slid open.

Thomas grinned. "Or you could open the door. What a surprise." He pushed past the silent but smug-looking Rick and went inside. "Come on, everyone. Somewhere in here there is evidence just waiting to clear our names."

He led them through the silent grounds to the main building where they'd decided it was most likely Chris had his private quarters—and the computer with the accurate records of his misdeeds.

Again they avoided the main doorway and instead found one of the smaller exits, although there were still plenty of serious locks there. And something else. Once Rick worked his magic and got them inside, they found themselves in a corridor made of some smooth material that gleamed in the dim light.

Curious, Harriet reached out to stroke the glossy white surface. It reminded her uncomfortably of a laboratory wall. She looked back over at Thomas who was frowning, his eyes dark with concern.

"This isn't good."

"What is it?"

"The plans called for biofilters but this is more than that. I think—" he paused. "This entryway reminds me of something you might have seen many years ago." He took a deep breath and looked grim. "During the last inter-system pandemic."

Harriet's heart stopped and, when it started beating again, went into overdrive. The last epidemic had been a horrible thing, nearly wiping out both normal humans and those with enhanced characteristics. In the decades that followed there'd been many attempts to manipulate vaccines to provide resistance to the hyperVs, as the biologically enhanced viruses had been dubbed. So desperate was the situation that many previously unthinkable projects had been given quiet approval, including the genetic modification program that had produced Harriet's ancestor, a blend of psi-powers in a robust werewolf package.

She was, in that sense, a product of the bio-wars.

Thomas continued to talk, his usual happy-go-lucky attitude notably absent. Harriet was reminded of just how old he must be, the first time she was really aware of his age and everything he'd experienced.

He pointed to slight indications in the walls at various heights. "These are decontamination sprayers. Someone coming in from the outside would stand in the mist until the sensors registered them as safe. The ceiling is filled with sensors and cameras that evaluate various light waves and chemical substances...that's why the walls are so smooth. Also..." He swallowed hard.

"If the sensors registered someone was running a fever or exhaling contaminants, they could be removed, sent back to the outside. A water cannon at the end of the corridor would wash them back through the door. Nothing to cling to...not that they'd be able to, once the gas got them."

"Gas?"

"The sprayers could be set up to deliver all kinds of things, not just a decontaminant. Depending on the morals—or desperation—of the operator, the system could incapacitate or kill. Either way, a convenient way to remove people you didn't want entering your facility."

Harriet chilled at the deadly quiet in his voice. "You saw all that?"

Thomas said nothing for a moment then shook his head sharply as if that would dislodge bad memories. "It was a long time ago. Nothing like that happens anymore, and it's even more unlikely with the new self-adapting vaccines."

She cocked a brow at him in inquiry. "Self-adapting? They've been around a while. All our field operatives have been inoculated."

"So have we. Costs a bundle to keep us up to date. They're not new, but there's a new iteration. Just came on the market a few months back. Scheduled to be out more than a year ago but some last-minute glitch held up approval. This one is supposed to work for everyone, even individuals sensitive to the older versions. The weakness of the early iterations was that they were live vaccines. A considerable segment of the population couldn't tolerate the vaccine itself and thus were at risk for developing the disease." He now sounded like a professor, discussing biochemistry instead of history. "There hasn't been an epidemic in over a hundred years. Miracles of modern science in terms of treatments but also sheer dumb luck. Every time we contact a new race or a new planet, we're playing with fire."

Elvie's voice sounded from the handheld. "Tommy, cut it short. We've got a job to do. In and out before anyone knows we're here, remember?"

"Okay, sorry." He shot a look at Harriet. "I'll give you the low-down later, if you're interested."

"Not me, I've heard it before." Rick softened his comment with a cheeky grin over his shoulder and went back to working on the inner door. "You never turn down a chance to lecture."

Thomas brushed aside Rick's objection. "We're carrying a shipment of the latest vaccine in our cargo hold, for one of the pioneer planets." He waved a hand around them. "I'm sure there's another explanation for what this looks like. If Elvie hadn't found the building permits, I'd think your boss had taken over one of those old survivalist facilities. Maybe he just copied the design."

While they talked, Rick had been busy. The door at the end of the hallway snicked open and he turned. "Time to go, folks. We should be past the worst of the alarms until we find your boss's private rooms, Harriet."

Thomas grinned, removing the years she'd suddenly seen in his face. Once again he was the boyish vampire she'd fallen in love with. "Sure, Rick. Let's go see how ol' Chris is spending our money!"

They left the cold sterile chamber behind, but Harriet couldn't quite get rid of the chill inside her. The thought of Christian having his hand on the controls of what Thomas described was something she didn't want to contemplate.

The rest of the building wasn't nearly as creepy in spite of the low-level maintenance lights glowing in the ceiling and how empty it was. Elvie warned them not to turn on any lights or cause a disruption in the flow of power that might alert one of the AIs.

Each room they came into was completed, furniture moved in and supplies in place. Everything was there—except for the people. The supplies and even the fixtures were arranged neatly, still in boxes and under wraps, so it was apparent no one had ever lived there. When those people did show up, they would have whatever they needed waiting for them, from a modern medical facility and entertainment centers to dining facilities—they found three of those, in different areas that could be separated by sealed bulkheads—and so many bedrooms Harriet lost count.

It made her wonder just how Christian would pick the ones to join him in his little fortress away from home. Somehow she doubted his current wife would be included and she knew he had no children.

As long as she'd known him, he hadn't been a family kind of guy.

Elvie directed them up and down stairs, through the labyrinth of passages. Twice they had to detour around an area governed by an AI she couldn't counter.

They explored until they finally found a door on the third level that they couldn't simply open. This, according to the map Elvie had downloaded to the handheld, must be where Chris' private quarters were.

It took Rick a particularly long time to disable all the safeguards and locks. This confirmed they had found the innermost sanctum, the holiest of holies for their nemesis.

Which made what appeared to their eyes as soon as the door opened especially remarkable.

"Gule's fleck!" Thomas stared in open wonder at the room. "It's a freaking sexcapade store!"

Equally stunned, Harriet and Rick stepped into a maze of shelves.

Thomas was right. The place looked like a warehouse, stocked with sexual paraphernalia. Whips. Chains. Everything from delicate tickler rings made of feathers to dildos whose size would have done a donkey proud. The three of them spread out among the aisles and shelves, wide-eyed, occasionally making noises of surprise and admiration.

Harriet sorted through the sexual riches and picked up a delicate leather outfit of blood-red straps and lace inlays. It shook out to an enticing cat suit that highlighted a woman's important parts. Behind it on the shelf lay a matching set of scarlet ropes, shackles with lots of shiny gold buckles and a book. She opened the plain cover and found the title page. *Manual of Bondage Techniques, Volume One*, published by the Intergalactic Fetish Society. Christian was proving to have some interesting, if somewhat disturbing, hobbies.

She held the outfit up. It would look pretty good on her. "Well, I guess that settles whether the current Mrs. Balhooey will be invited to this end-of-civilization-as-we-know-it party. She's not likely to fit into this little thing." None of the garments on the shelf would fit a lady of her generous proportions.

"You don't think he's planning on bringing his wife here? Naughty, naughty Harriet, to think he's got a squeeze on the side. If the woman married him, she'd certainly enjoy all this." Thomas stared around the room. "I'm not sure I've even heard of some of this stuff before. And it takes a lot to surprise me."

"There's so much of it," Rick said. "It would take years to use every one of these."

"Decades," Thomas added.

"What's in these?" Rick opened a couple of cartons in the corner. "Oh I see. Lube." He held up one tube then another. "Lube, lube…and more lube!" He held a couple of them closer to his goggles. "Hey, it's my favorite brand. And a new flavor!" The tubes disappeared into one of his coverall pockets.

"Now, remember, we aren't here to steal," Harriet told him, the leather garment still in her hand. When he turned to her, she hid it behind her back, reluctant to put it down. "All we want is the data that will clear you."

"Point taken," Thomas nodded, but he didn't tell his partner to put the lube back. "Let's be careful to leave everything as we found it."

Rick resealed the cartons and pushed them back into the corner. "One thing about it, your boss is planning on being here more than a few years. It would take a decade to go through all this, even if a dozen couples were living here."

Harriet agreed with his assessment and, uneasy with the picture she was putting together, followed them out of the room. The Christian Balhooey she knew wouldn't be willing to give up his social status unless he had no choice. Seeing this place made her wonder just what would have to happen to make hiding out here a necessity. She found herself echoing Thomas' words.

This isn't good.

The next door secured by layers of locks slid open to reveal pitch-black space. Thomas frowned. "Elvie, there are no maintenance lights in here."

"I can detect no fixtures for emergency lighting, Tommy. You'll have to make your own."

They switched on their handhelds, set to low. Rick fastened one to his sleeve and concentrated on giving Elvie a good view of what they found.

Thomas flashed his to high and swept it across the room before they moved in. The doorway led to a huge entertainment room and beyond that, the most sumptuous bedroom they'd seen so far. Harriet used the word "entertainment" loosely. The room was more of a dungeon, in the most sexual connotation imaginable. The sexcapade storage room was obviously meant to supply the activities carried out in here.

Strategically placed hooks dangled from the ceiling and were mounted along the walls. There were slings, shackles, platforms of all heights and tables laid with all manner of stimulants, both physical and chemical, and appliances. Vibrators, dildos, anal beads, instant hot and cold packs in odd sizes and shapes, gags, whips, candles, clips and clamps, floggers, ticklers and so much lube it made Harriet wonder just how many people Chris was planning on having at hand—and of what gender.

Or what species...on one bench there were even a few restraints made of silver alloy that weren't coated the way hers were. Not only would they restrain a werewolf or vampire, they'd burn the skin. Harriett shuddered. Nasty stuff.

These were the only two rooms in the whole compound that showed any signs of occupation. Some of the tubes and pots of cream were partially used. Harriet examined the array of items on a large table. Handles on several of the tools had the embossed lettering almost worn off. The leather straps on a couple of shackles were no longer new, pliable and marked where the buckles had been worked.

Thomas opened a sealed cupboard. He stepped back and moaned. "Oh gods, there's blood here, old blood. Lots of it."

Harriet directed her handheld over his shoulder and the light gleamed off a collection of the more sinister type of sex toy, featuring spikes and pins and blades. She got a shock when Thomas turned his back on the contents. He'd grown pale and his hand shook when he lifted it to swipe at his hair. The pupils of his eyes were large and glowing.

Rick opened up a link, sweeping Harriet into a three-way connection. *We'll have to help him control himself. Don't take too long.* The two of them partially merged with the vampire, tamping down the blood lust and controlling his reaction.

"I think we can safely say that Chris-kid is not a nice guy." Elvie's voice was tart.

"I figured that out when I realized he was the one trying to kill us," Harriet pointed out. She pushed the cupboard doors closed and secured them.

"And steal our ship," Rick added. "Let's get a move on before Thomas loses it."

In the low illumination provided by her handheld, Harriet stared down the long room. Taken in its entirety, it was both frightening and arousing. She could imagine herself spread-eagled on the wall, straining against her bonds while Rick and Thomas teased her mercilessly. Her pussy heated until she remembered this was where her boss brought his squeezes, as Thomas had called them.

She didn't like Christian. She never had and this trip was revealing far more than she'd ever wanted to know about him. The thought of her pudgy, domineering boss—or even worse, that slimy rat Giles—wielding the blades Thomas had found was like a dash of icy water between her shoulder blades.

"So this *is* where he comes on those trips," Harriet murmured. "I'd wondered."

"Okay, I've got a data center here," Rick called out.

Harriet pulled her attention away from trying to decide where she'd hide something she wanted to keep secret and found him in the bedroom. Ignoring the silk pillows and the rumpled giant four-poster bed someone had neglected to make up, she and Thomas crowded behind Rick.

"Elvie, can you trace any connections to this location?"

"Nope, no cables leading there from any of the main systems. Just power feeds. Guys, it looks to be an isolated system. That makes it likely to be what we're looking for."

Rick examined the unit, careful not to touch anything. "Doesn't look like it's booby-trapped."

"Are there any data crystals or disks lying around? There might be backups that would be easier to make off with," Elvie pointed out. "The more I see of this place, the less I like you being in there. The sooner you're out, the better. Now show me what you found."

While Rick held the tablet so Elvie could get a direct visual of the data center, Harriet and Thomas fanned out to search the room. Elvie and Rick mumbled in the background. Thomas opened the closet and began pawing through pockets and shoes.

Sorting through a jumble of stuff in the bedside table, Harriet came across the most darling vibrator she'd ever seen. The variety of extensions and a remote control all fit into a neat little case. What was even more appealing about it was that the seal on the case was intact...this was a toy that Chris hadn't gotten around to using.

Without saying anything, she slid it into a pocket. Too bad that red cat suit wasn't smaller. She would have rather had that, but beggars—well, to be honest they were more like thieves—couldn't be choosers.

She wouldn't take anything else here. No telling where it had been. The very thought of what her boss did on his off hours, and with whom, made her shudder. She did not want to go there.

Through the link, she felt Thomas begin to relax. Removal from the source of his temptation must reduce the voracious urge he felt to feed. The need that had pricked at her ebbed and she relaxed.

Until his excitement flared up, pure golden light that outshone both her mind and Rick's. "Got something here! I'll bet it's exactly what we need."

He turned around to face them and held up a small box. The transparent top revealed more than a dozen tiny data crystals fitted into padded slots. "It was behind a false panel at the back of a lower shelf."

"Let me check." Rick hurried over, holding up the unit to let Elvie see.

They stood, holding their breath, until the AI spoke again. "Yes, I've got a reader for those in the spare parts workshop. Bring 'em on back and we'll see what we can do."

"What if they're not what we want?" Thomas asked.

"I thought we were going to copy what we need and leave the originals." Rick snapped the handheld shut. "As in no one will know we were here."

"I'm not sure it matters now," Elvie said. "One of the AIs has been monitoring your presence but so far has chosen to do nothing. No signals have gone out, no warnings and no implementation of the security measures." There was a slight pause. "I think he's sweet on me." Harriet had to smile at the feminine satisfaction in her voice.

"Either that, or he knows more than we do and has a conscience." Thomas slid the panel back into place and returned the clothing to the shelf. "The more I see of this, the more worried I am. This guy has built a sterile fortress. He's planned on getting our ship for months or more."

Something snapped into place in Harriet's brain. The connection she'd been trying to make for hours. A chill ran up her spine and her fingers half-turned into claws. She fisted her hands and willed the fury away. Much as she suddenly wanted to shred Chris' bedroom, wanton destruction would do nothing but delay them.

"No, he hasn't. I think the reason you never got any late notices is because your delinquency is a construct he threw together by manipulating the system and altering old entries. Yes, he's been building a secure bolt-hole here for some time but I'll bet the *Sleepwalker* is a recent element in his plan. Don't you see?"

Rick looked at her, horror dawning in his face. "The vaccine?"

"Christian has severe allergies." She turned to Thomas. "You said approval was delayed and you've got one of the first shipments. Given all the attention to detail in this place I'd expect there to be some stockpiled here, but that's one thing I don't recall seeing in that med station we went through."

"Let's check before we jump to conclusions. We weren't looking at the supplies that closely."

The three of them hastily put things back as close to where they'd found them as they could. When all the doors they'd found closed were shut again, they hotfooted it back out, threading their way through the twists and turns of hallways and stairwells, back to the infirmary.

Somewhere along the way, they made a wrong turn. Harriet didn't notice until Elvie shouted at them to stop just as Thomas barreled through a door. There was no way he could stop. Harriet watched in horror as the hatch slammed shut behind Thomas, leaving her and Rick alone. The maintenance lights flickered and an alarm sounded.

Rick turned to her. She could see his worried eyes behind the goggles. Opening up the link they all shared, she called out, *Thomas?*

Yeah? Hey, the door closed and I can't open it.

Hang on, we'll try to get it open from this side.

Rick examined the hatch for some kind of handle then turned his attention to the walls nearby, looking for a panel he could access.

The shrill bwoop-bwoop cut out. The following silence was worse than the noise.

"Rick!" The AI's voice was strained.

"Yes, Elvie?"

"I'm under attack by the AIs. Open up the ceiling right above your side of that door and sever the largest conduit."

Sweet Sol, what next? Harriet again contacted Thomas. *You'll have to wait a bit longer. Elvie needs our help.*

He didn't respond immediately. She kept the link open so she'd know if he reached out, and paid attention to what was going on right in front of her.

Abandoning the door, Rick reached up and thrust his fist into the cavity above them. He pulled down a portion of the ceiling in a shower of dust and rubble to reveal a space filled with cables and pipes. Holding up the tablet, he aimed the viewer into the hole.

"It's buried inside a bundle of stuff. Do you have the fusion drill I gave you?"

"No, Thomas has it. He's on the other side of that door."

Elvie made a sound of frustration. "I'm barely holding him off and I detect a massive power surge he's trying to force through."

"Which one do you need severed?" Rick frowned at the confusion of utility cables. Harriet moved closer to see into the dark cavity.

"There's a blue conduit inside that bundle to the left. But be careful—the main power cable is right beside it." Her voice broke up in a crackle of static and the comm device went silent.

Rick stretched up again and tried to get his hand around it—and failed. Supersynth tie-wraps held the entire collection flush against the ceiling. The bundle was too big for him to get a grip on the whole thing and too tight for him to pick out just the comm feed.

Harriet didn't hesitate. Elvie was their only chance of making it out of here and contacting Bernie. If the AI was taken over, they'd all be in mortal danger. She marked which cable was the one she wanted, counting over to it and noting its size.

She slipped off her coveralls and stood naked in the hallway. Panic made the change come faster. Her fingers lengthened and grew thicker. Her mouth elongated into a muzzle. With the popping of joints and a wrench in her vision, Harriet dropped down on four paws.

Color faded and the pipes and conduits all looked alike to her werewolf vision but she picked out the one she wanted just before she leapt upward. She shouldered Rick out of the way and turned her head sideways. Eyes riveted on her quarry, she dug her fangs into the thick cables.

The low power running through the data cable tickled her teeth as she snapped it. Her jaws closed a little too far though, and one fang penetrated the sheathing on the neighboring cable. A surge of electricity seared her mouth.

Rick watched in horror as Harriet fell back in a shower of sparks. Damnation, first Thomas got cut off from them and now this.

He jumped forward and half-caught her, dropping the handheld. His stance was awkward and he couldn't hold her but at least she didn't hit the floor at full force. Tendrils of smoke rose from her mouth and sparks continued to drop from the opening in the ceiling. He dragged the dead weight of her wolf form out from under the hole.

Thomas! He needed help.

The door swung open. "Yes?" Thomas stepped through. "What the hell?"

Rick didn't waste energy on speaking aloud. He opened up their link and shared what he'd seen. *She did it to save Elvie. I think she hit the power cable.*

Thomas hunkered beside Harriet and touched her face. "Her pulse is strong but unsteady. She just nicked it or she'd be dead."

Rick grabbed the handheld and poked at it. "Elvie?"

Nothing but silence answered him. He thumbed a button and nothing happened. No lights blinked, no sensors beeped.

"Elvie?"

"Yes, Ricky?" Elvie's voice sounded from all around them.

"You're intact!"

"So it appears." Her tart tone turned into a simper. "I have my friend Guvnor to thank for that. He stopped Mallet's attempt to overpower me."

"And don't forget Harriet. She bit through the cable."

Thomas broke in. "We'll sort this out later. Elvie, Harriet's in shock and needs medical attention. We've got to get out of here."

"I suggest you take her to the med station you were heading for and get help for her there. That will let you finish your mission." She added, "Oh and don't worry about any restrictions on where you can go. Mallet's been contained for the moment. He won't hamper your progress again."

Thomas lifted Harriet and carried her to the infirmary, Rick behind him, her coverall in his hands. Rick winced when they hit a doorframe or brushed against the walls but each time Thomas assured him, "She's out cold and can't feel it." He already knew that but it bothered him anyway.

Lights sprang on ahead of them and doors snicked open as they reached them. Elvie kept up a running commentary.

"I've got access to all kinds of stuff here. You were absolutely right about Chris-kid having a number of different identities. I've inventoried the infirmary supplies. You'll find stim packs on the right and bandages on the top shelf in the closet. Healing ointment is with the bandages."

"Elvie, we'll use the stim packs but I've got everything else I need in my mouth."

"Oh."

Rick suppressed a chuckle. Elvie had forgotten Thomas had vampire saliva, with all its healing powers. That meant she was concerned for Harriet, and no one would ever convince him she wasn't. He shared that thought with Thomas as they entered the medical facility.

I only hope you're right, the vampire said as he slapped a stim packet onto Harriet's side. She stirred and they immediately realized she'd not been quite as out of it as expected.

Yeah, I'll believe Elvie's concern when I see it. Harriet's mental voice was much stronger than he expected.

How are you doing?

I feel like a wormhole opened up in my nose and I must have twisted my leg when I fell.

They set her on the exam table.

No, the floor.

Huh?

I'm afraid I'll fall off when I shift.

Do you want me to heal you now or after you change form?

She hesitated.

Rick and Thomas exchanged glances. They shared Harriet's pain. Rick knew what it cost Thomas to remain calm and keep his tone light. He was getting frustrated himself as seconds ticked off. Seconds that they were all hurting.

Harriet, honey, I don't mind licking your furry face.

Her relief flooded the link. *You don't?*

I imagine changing will be easier if you're whole. Won't it? She was silent. *What are you worried about — that I'll get hair stuck in my teeth? It can't be worse than Rick's balls.* The vampire stroked a thumb over her cheek. *You're a lot softer. In all the right places.*

Okay. You're right. She still didn't sound comfortable about them handling her while she was in her wolf form but she'd agreed. Rick let out the breath he hadn't realized he'd been holding. That meant they'd get back to the safety of the *Sleepwalker* soon.

Pretty wolfie. You'd better get well soon, so I can lick you somewhere else. Thomas spoke gently to her through their link. He stroked her ruff with one hand as he laved her muzzle with his healing saliva. The swelling subsided and damaged skin flaked off under his ministrations. By the time he lifted his head, her wolf face appeared normal.

She struggled to her feet, leapt off the table and shook. For the first time, Rick could admire her completely.

Like her hair in her human form, her coat was black, streaked and tipped with gold. She stood waist-high to him at her shoulders, which made her fairly large for a female wolf. Intelligent golden eyes stared at him from a sturdy face, atop a broad chest. She was built for power and speed.

He'd hate to face her in battle.

If you want to turn around, I'm going to change. As much as she tried to hide it, they both heard the expectation of rejection in her voice.

No way. I want to watch! Thomas had regained his normal enthusiasm.

Yeah, if we're going to be together for a while, we need to know what's normal for you.

You're sure?

When they both nodded, she gave them a doggy grin, tossed her head and began to shift.

Once she stood before them in her glorious human form, Rick could see that her face hadn't healed completely. Angry red marks showed where the current had seared the flesh, although there was little swelling.

She touched her jaw gingerly and winced. "Not bad, considering how it felt a few minutes ago." She took a step and stumbled.

Thomas caught her. "Don't go too fast. We've got a lot of ground to cover and you've had quite a shock."

Rick raised his eyebrows. "Pun intended?"

Thomas twisted his lips into a grimace. "No, but I'll take it."

After donning her coverall, Harriet took a shaky step toward the cabinets around them. "Now let's see what's in stock here. Weren't we looking for vaccines?"

"We'll look. You sit and recover." Rick told her.

They turned to survey the contents of the cabinets. Sure enough, there was no vaccine at all, not even any older, disease-specific ones. An empty space gaped on a shelf, next to an array of standard pharmaceutical preparations.

Rick swallowed as the tiny spark of hope that he was wrong died. "As if he expected to have need for just one kind."

"Let's get out of here." Harriet's voice was flat.

"If you need more data, you can always get in again," Elvie reminded them. "Guvnor's on our side, so it'll be a walk in the park. We won't leave orbit until we know we have what we came for."

"I think we got more than we expected."

Chapter Ten

෨

The flight back to the *Sleepwalker* was tense. Still shaken from their near escape and the pain of her injuries, Harriet leaned back in her rear seat as Rick piloted the small shuttle, Thomas in the copilot seat next to him. The vampire's face was paler than ever and his lips were drawn back, revealing his fangs.

He seemed to be trying to stay focused on the space around them, but she watched him give surreptitious glances at Rick...and Rick's neck.

She could smell his need...arousal and hunger poured off him in waves. After exposure to the old blood on Chris' "toys", plus the intensity of the fight to save Elvie, Thomas had reached a breaking point.

He needed blood—and sex, and he needed them now.

Harriet checked their progress. Fifteen minutes until they reached the ship. Surely Thomas could make it that long...

I'm not going to make it. She felt as much as heard that mental cry. The vampire was in full bloodlust now, his eyes gleaming red with pent-up frustration, his mind ablaze with sensual need. With soothing words, Rick offered his wrist. "Drink—take what you need."

Not enough...need all *of you!*

"Harriet, can you pilot?" Rick's voice was a low sensual growl that pulled her out of her own misery and into full arousal. Ignoring that, plus her pain, she struggled out of her seatbelt and pushed between the front seats into the shuttle's tiny cockpit.

Thomas' eyes glowed as she approached and for an instant she wondered if she'd be the focus of the vampire's hunger, but Rick pushed her into the seat he'd just vacated.

As she took over the controls, the two men embraced and tumbled into the small cargo space back of the seats.

The inside of the cockpit window was as reflective as a mirror and as Harriet guided the shuttle back to the *Sleepwalker*, she could see Thomas and Rick, struggling with each other's clothes, not bothering to undo everything, just enough to release their cocks, fully engorged and weeping. Then they were locked in an embrace, rubbing themselves together. Sexuality ran off them and filled the small space of the shuttle.

Harriet's clit swelled and her pussy flooded, but she forced herself to stay focused on the job at hand. She had to get them back to the *Sleepwalker* and safety—and then she'd bang their brains out.

In the reflective window it looked like a wrestling match, both men heavily involved. Thomas' hands flew over Rick's suit, patting down the pockets. "Lube, lube…where is the frackin' lube?"

Rick's laugh sounded forced. "Here." He shoved a tube into the other man's hands and braced himself against the wall as Thomas stripped the suit away from his back, baring it and his ass. The vampire took a quick moment to apply lube to his cock before he pushed his way into Rick's anus. His entry wasn't slow the way Thomas would normally be, savoring it, careful to cause no harm. This wasn't the gentle vampire Harriet knew but a desperate creature, near feral in its need.

Feral in the way he fucked his friend, and in the way his teeth dug into Rick's back. Thomas was in his vampire heart here, overcome by the situation they'd just lived through. He could no longer help himself, any more than Harriet could stop turning furry under the influence of a planetary moon.

Here he was truly himself. Harriet found it near appalling...and extremely exciting. After the way he'd accepted her in her wolf form, something no other person had ever done, she couldn't do less for him.

She wished it was her body he was using so thoroughly but knew that Rick had prior claim, as well as the knowledge of what their vampire partner needed. She could only watch and direct the slow-moving shuttle toward their ship.

Behind her the action grew more intense and even though she faced forward, she couldn't help what she heard and even more what her mind sensed. She felt their gold and purple mental essences flow together, matching in their wild swirl the intensity of their bodies' coupling. It was mad and intense, and she felt Thomas' hunger as if it were her own.

She couldn't help reaching for them and taking some of that into herself. The sensation was so strong she could almost taste Rick's blood. It was good, and the pull Thomas used to suck it grew more intense.

Too intense. Harriet could also feel Rick, his mind overcome with sex and need, his body taking the near punishing coupling from Thomas with ease but his heart resisted the pull on his veins. Not much longer until it would falter as Thomas sucked the life out of him.

The purple in their combined minds weakened and paled.

Too much blood, taken too fast. This was what they'd mentioned, what happened when they were both so wound up. Keeping most of her attention on her piloting, she let her mind reach to them, covering their purple and gold in a green haze, calming them.

Enough, Thomas. You've taken enough...

Thomas stopped sucking, for a moment breathing hard against Rick's back. In her mind Harriet felt his awareness return. He quickly sealed the wounds, wiping them clean. He reached around and grabbed Rick's cock and began a furious pumping on it, the movement of his hips speeding up.

Rick groaned and his body jerked as he came in Thomas' hand.

The proximity bell grabbed Harriet's attention and she activated the set of controls to start the docking procedure. Behind her there was another groan and gasp as Thomas finally found completion. Their reflections showed their embrace and a kiss that looked like an apology on Thomas' part. That was confirmed by his whispered "I'm sorry" that Harriet's werewolf hearing picked up.

She finished the docking, so smooth their shuttle didn't even jerk as it halted and was swept into the recessed docking bay. The door slid shut, closing off the view of the planet. As the external pressure equalized with that of the *Sleepwalker*, the hatch opened with an audible click.

Harriet turned to see both men staring at her, their clothes disheveled but back more or less where they should be.

"You saved my life," Rick said quietly. "Again."

"And mine. I wouldn't have survived if I'd hurt him. And you saved Elvie back there," Thomas added.

They both stepped toward her. Harriet felt the weight of their minds and sexual interest. The release they'd had in the back of the shuttle, intense as it was, had just taken the edge off.

She made as if to move toward the door and Thomas was there immediately, between her and it. Stars, vampires could move quickly when they wanted.

He gave her a toothy grin, his fangs prominent. "Oh yes we can."

Rick came up behind her, trapping her between them. "I think we need a little down time." He spoke into the comm-unit. "Elvie, there's a package of data crystals here from the hideout. Send a 'bot down here to collect it."

"Aren't you coming to the bridge?" Harriet thought the AI sounded almost hurt and faintly annoyed.

"Not yet." Rick's eyes met Harriet's and she nearly melted from the heat of his stare. "Got something to take care of."

She tried to back away, but they moved together and Harriet found herself sandwiched between the two men. Two hard-bodied and very aroused men.

Rick turned her toward him and leaned forward to kiss her. There was no apology in this kiss—it was all male possession. Behind her Thomas moved in and began nuzzling her neck. Hands traced her curves under her pants and jacket. Whose hands they were was no longer important to her.

If what they were doing to her body wasn't enough, both were also assaulting her with their minds. Purple and gold thoughts entwined with hers, thoughts full of flesh and blood, and bodies as intimately involved as possible.

Already aroused by their experiences on the moon and from witnessing the two men making love, Harriet's sex drive launched into hyperspeed.

"I need you," she whispered to no one in particular.

"Good." She heard Rick's voice, but Thomas echoed the sentiment in her mind. Rick was the one who swept her up in his arms and carried her from the shuttle, Thomas in hot pursuit.

We need you too.

Harriet considered pointing out that she was capable of walking to the cabin, particularly since she could feel Rick's weakness from blood loss, but the man didn't seem interested in arguing about it. He walked so fast that Thomas had to trot to keep up with him, and again she was reminded of just how strong he was. All that time spent in zero-Gs, pumping to stay as fit as his vampire buddy.

She could have jumped from his arms but she realized he was trying to make a point. She'd rescued him and now he wanted to carry her. She'd go along with it for the moment.

Besides, it felt really good being carried by this man. He smelled so good, of both himself and Thomas, and the smell of great sex as well. If Thomas had been feral before, now it seemed to have rubbed off on Rick, and Harriet realized she was reacting to both of them. Both dominant males to her innate female.

Both dominant, physically as well as sexually. She was in for one wild ride tonight—and she could hardly wait.

When they reached their rooms, Rick moved unerringly toward his quarters, punching the door's control with a fist. He strode to the bed and placed Harriet gently in the center. With a smooth movement he pulled off his shirt and slid onto the bed next to her.

Thomas followed him inside and pulled on his shirt tabs to open it, sliding it from his shoulders. But when he hurried to join them, Rick held up his hand.

He stared pointedly at his friend's crotch. "Don't you think you better clean up?"

Thomas followed his gaze and if anything appeared to blush. "I'll be right back. Don't start without me." The last was almost plaintive as he palmed open the door to the sanitary.

Rick's lips twitched as he pulled Harriet into his arms. "At last we're alone."

"Aren't we going to wait for Thomas?"

With two pulls he had her shirt off and on the floor next to his. "You really want to wait?"

"Uh, no…" Harriet's voice trailed off as he dipped his head between her now bared breasts. She whimpered as he took one nipple into his mouth, suckling it hard before leaning to grin up at her.

"I didn't think so. Thomas can catch up." He nuzzled her breast again. "Me, I need you now."

And she needed him badly.

He continued to worship her breasts until she was nearly frantic. "More, Rick."

"More the lady wants, more the lady shall have." He pulled off her pants and slid her to the edge of the bed. Kneeling on the floor between her legs, he leaned into her crotch and breathed in deeply through his nose.

"Gule's fleck, but you smell good. I can't believe I went so long without enjoying a woman's smell."

Suddenly curious, she asked. "How long?"

"Years. Many, many years. We were in space, we had each other. I didn't miss it." He stared up at her and she saw something very earnest in his eyes. "I would miss you."

Something about the way he said it caught her attention, even through the sensual haze that engulfed her. He said he would miss her… as if there was some possibility she wouldn't be moving on once their troubles were straightened out.

For the first time she got the distinct impression that Thomas and Rick had plans for her that extended much farther into the future than she'd considered. She thought briefly of saying something but Rick's mouth closed over her pussy, his tongue sliding along the thin folds to find her clit, touching it briefly, and all questions fled her mind.

For a man who barely remembered what a woman smelled like, Rick sure knew his way around oral sex with one. He murmured something about loving her taste as he proceeded to lick every centimeter of her with obsessive concentration. Harriet let go of her worries and writhed beneath him as a wave of orgasmic delight built inside her. It finally crashed over her and she screamed out her pleasure. When he went to dip back into her, she caught his head.

"Too much…need to rest."

Rick leaned up on one elbow and grinned at her. "I brought a little something from your old boss' stash of goodies." From a pocket he produced a narrow bottle labeled "sensor-lube".

A tiny dab of the clear gel on his finger and he swept it across her clit. Somewhere between fire and ice, the sensation was like a warming lube—pleasantly sensual but not too much. Just enough to keep her terribly turned on.

Not that she really needed it…but it was very, very pleasant.

Between gasps, she reached for her jacket. "I found a toy too." She pulled out the vibrator with its attachments and Rick's face lit up as he opened the case.

"Cool! There's a really nice anal plug in here." He eyed her with sudden inspiration. "Give me a moment with this," and he took the box, leaving her wanting attention.

Fortunately, the door to the sanitary slid open. "I thought you were going to wait!"

Harriet looked over at Thomas, lounging naked in the doorway, a disappointed look on his face and his freshly washed cock in hand, hard and ready. Just what she needed — a horny vampire!

"You asked but we never agreed." She grinned at him, showing all her sharp teeth. "Get over here, Thomas. We may have started without you, but no way are we finished. Rick just got me warmed up."

He grinned back and practically leapt from the doorway onto the bed next to her. When he checked out what Rick was playing with, he laughed. "I see someone else broke that 'don't take anything' rule." He got to his feet and headed back to the bathroom, returning with his jacket, fumbling in the pocket. "I had it here someplace…"

Out came a box with a collection of nipple clamps, cock rings and assorted other small goodies. Who'd been using those, she wondered.

"Not to worry," Thomas said, obviously reading her expression. "I got them from a sealed box." He picked up a clamp, sniffed it and smiled. "Completely unused."

Behind her came a small buzzing noise. "This is new too. Still in the case."

Harriet sighed. So much for keeping a low profile. Hopefully with everything there, no one would notice a few missing items.

"I came to haul your asses in for nonpayment and instead you turn me into a thief!" She gave him an exaggerated frown. "You really are very bad."

"Not bad," Thomas said. "Just rogues. No one gets hurt by our actions. We're naughty but nice...and we're playful." He caressed her bare nipple with the clamp, letting the cold metal chill her skin.

"Very playful," Rick added, using the vibrating narrow tip of one of the attachments on her other breast. "And you've just become our favorite playmate."

She certainly felt played with, between her clit tingling from the gel and the attentions of both men on her nipples. Harriet rose up on her hands and knees and reached for Thomas, who happened to have the nearest cock. "Come here, neglected one. I want to play with you."

He sighed as her mouth closed over the tip of his cock. He tasted clean and fresh with a hint of soap. Barely a trace of his own scent came through, but that was enough to push her arousal to new heights. She sucked on him hard, and he groaned his pleasure. "Gule's fleck, that's good."

Not to be outdone, he tugged gently on her nipple, elongating it before fitting the clamp over it. The sensation was similar to a man's suckling, but for a continuous stretch of time. While she whimpered over that, he found a matching clamp and performed the same task on her other nipple.

A pleasurable ache grew from both nipples, spreading down to her core, filling her with anticipation. Harriet moaned and found it hard to keep her attention focused on sucking Thomas' cock.

Behind her, Rick was manipulating the little vibrator he'd found all along her neck and shoulders, leaving trails of sensitized nerves in its wake. She had to be impressed by the skill he had with the toy, given how he'd just gotten his hands on it. Apparently it wasn't his first experience with such a device. No wonder he'd grabbed it so quickly.

Now he let it drift to the small of her back, running it along her spine and to the tender spot just at the base. Not quite into the split of her buttocks but almost. A teasing place from which the vibrations set up a thrill deep inside her. The growing ache from the clamps on her nipples fed that thrill.

It was a very short journey to the place she knew he was headed, her virgin anal passage. He'd told her before how he was interested in fucking—no, that's not what he'd said—making love to her there. Using a toy would be the first step toward what he wanted.

Harriet took Thomas' cock from her mouth to turn her head and look at Rick. He stared back at her. In her mind she heard him.

If it is all right with you?

A delicious shudder ran through her, in part that he wanted her permission and in part that she was being so stimulated by these incredible men and their purloined toys. Well, she'd always been a little curious about it and certainly watching the guys get off that way had been exciting. *Just use plenty of lube.*

Of course!

His enthusiastic mental shout almost hurt, but she grinned as he grabbed one of his stolen tubes and laughed when he made a point of tasting the contents.

He rolled his eyes. "Mmm, yummy."

"In that case, pass it when you're done." She indicated Thomas' cock in her hand. "I could use a condiment."

"My cock is not a food item…" Thomas said, his voice breaking off into an appreciative hiss as she again closed her mouth over him. She scraped her sharp teeth across the sensitive head and he moaned. "Oh gods, forget that, you can eat me all you want."

She felt the tube slip into her hand, but before she could do anything with it, another sensation caught her attention. The little vibrator had moved to her rear opening and was gently teasing its way in. Rick had no trouble pushing it past the muscular ring. Small and well lubed, with the flared outer edge keeping it from slipping completely inside, it soon rested firmly in her.

For a moment she just savored the oddity of the feeling, of being filled from behind, even by such a small item. It vibrated just enough to keep her aware of its presence. Rick's hands massaged her bottom, adding to the sensation.

He lifted her higher up on her knees and reached forward to play with her clit, still slick and tingling from the sensitizing lube he'd used. She felt his cock behind her, hard and probing at her pussy. As she moaned around Thomas' cock, Rick entered her, taking his time.

He pushed in and out of her with deliberate slowness, making her cry out more than once. All orifices filled, Harriet barely hung on to sanity.

Then the anal plug sped up courtesy of the remote control in Rick's hand and sanity became a lost goal. Harriet reached orgasm again, harder than before and accidentally bit down on Thomas' cock, drawing a little blood which she was careful not to swallow. They had enough bloodsucking going on around here and she had no desire to become the first vampire werewolf on record. She was pretty sure being a werewolf already made her immune to the DNA changes that would turn her into a vampire. On the other hand, it hadn't kept her from being psychic so who knew what else she might be susceptible to.

Thomas echoed her concern. "Careful. I do all the biting around here." His tone was joking, but she knew he was right.

"Maybe we better switch around then. Hard to keep my teeth to myself," she gasped out, releasing Thomas' cock.

"Hear that, Rick?" Thomas said. "Move. My turn in her pussy."

Rick narrowed his eyes. "I just got here."

"Then give me the remote for the vibrator."

Rick clutched it closer. "No way! I'm not giving up the remote."

"That's not fair. You've got all the best parts."

"There is nothing wrong with my mouth," Harriet protested.

Thomas gave her an exaggerated frown. "Your teeth are too sharp. You bit me."

"Only when I come...which, incidentally, I'm not doing now because you two are fighting instead of fucking." Harriet said, starting to get annoyed. She glanced at the vibrator case Rick had dropped on the bed. "Why don't you see what else you can find in there?"

Thomas looked and found a sheath that rolled down over his cock—and a larger vibrating butt plug. He was going to put it in himself but Rick held out his hand.

"You know you always need help with those." After careful lubing, he inserted it into his partner's ass.

Thomas made a long moan as it sank in to the flange. "Oh thanks, Rick. Now that feels *good*."

Rick picked up the remote and adjusted it for the new devices. "Wait until it's turned on."

In moments all three of them were moaning in unison. Thomas lay next to them, the sheath and butt vibrator doing their jobs while Rick took Harriet from behind, the nipple clamps still sending delicious thrills through her, as well as the gently vibrating plug buried in her ass.

With the extra help it didn't take long for all of them to finish.

Chapter Eleven

೮

"On another note, is it possible Chris-kid could be using the alias Cristina Smerkish?" Elvie's voice had returned to being chipper now that they'd finished "taking care of things" in the bedroom and arrived back on the bridge. She'd gone through the various disks, most of which had been deemed useless, but one had held a set of deeds and accounts with names she was cross-referencing.

Thomas laughed. "Oh, he's crossing genders now?"

"I know that name." Harriet held a hand up. "Wait a minute, it'll come to me. That's, that's, oh frag it, that's Giles' half-sister."

"Your little twerp from Sedilous?"

"The one and only. He and Chris have always been close. Don't tell me his whole family's involved."

"Whole family?" Rick asked.

"Tommy, Ricky, I've cross-referenced them in the ancestry database on Glavius Six. The Smerkish family is firmly tied to several of the leading crime families. Intermarrying for at least fifteen generations."

Both men stared at each other. "Uh-oh."

"Uh-oh is right," Harriet said. "I didn't know that. Elvie, where did you see Cristina's name?"

"She popped up several times on a search I conducted for Deltan, the destination colony for the vaccine we're carrying."

"Okay, I'll bite," Thomas said. "What's special about Deltan and how does that fit into the repossession of our ship?"

"Deltan is quite rich in a number of rare metals. The colony barely predates a mining claim by the Hooverville Company. Smerkish is listed as the broker on a number of stock transfers in that company as well as an author of the initial claim." There was a short pause before Elvie spoke again in a much less cocky tone. "Oh this is bad. This is very, very bad. I'm sending the results of my search to all terminals."

Silence descended on the bridge as data structures and associations flickered across the screens. The three rapidly scanned the information, taking in the magnitude and ramifications of what Elvie had put together.

"Damnation!"

Rick winced. Thomas only used that archaic term when he was profoundly upset. Even with his back to the others and no mental link, hunched over a data display, the anger radiating from the vampire pressed against his mind. He wasn't any less angry himself, but he was better at controlling strong emotions.

The Hooverville Company apparently was a joint project of two cooperating crime families. Although it was publicly traded, no outsiders sat on the board of directors and Cristina Smerkish brokered all stock transfers. All those commissions made it a sweet deal for her.

Geology reports from Deltan revealed that the planet held phenomenal deposits of blastema, the most rare metal yet discovered. Blastema, according to a recent scientific paper, could be used to vastly increase the speed and range of interstellar engines. The research projects underway at several universities promised to revolutionize space flight.

The planet's mining rights represented untold wealth.

Unfortunately for all the companies standing in line ready to bid, grant of those rights had been put on hold when the colony was established. As long as the colony was thriving, and until the colonial government was formed and stable enough to participate in the negotiations, no rights would be awarded.

The colony was made up of refugees from a solar system whose sun had gone nova several years ago. The survivors of the three inhabited planets in that system had pooled their resources and purchased the right to jointly colonize Deltan. By all reports, they were doing quite well at it. The edu-vid companies had produced numerous human-interest stories on the Deltans' success, profiling the way the disparate groups had hammered out their differences in cultures. They'd forged a single society, one that provided dignity to every member of the colony as well as freedom of religion, education, sexual and even parafolk equality.

So on one side was a group of hard-working and noble colonists. On the other were Christian and his crew of less-than-honorable cronies.

Working the family ties in the genealogy data, Elvie had pulled together a string of unconnected facts and tied them into an ugly pattern. These all centered around Giles, who they all now knew was a longtime friend of Chris Balhooey's.

Cristina Smerkish worked for the brokerage firm specializing in, among other companies owned by the crime families, Hooverville stock. Giles Taylor worked for Galaxy Financial.

But the most disturbing information was that Giles had another half-sibling, a brother with an entirely different surname. That man had worked as a bio-researcher for a lab under investigation for a number of laboratory animals that had disappeared.

Those specific animals had been infected with an experimental bio-terror virus—fast-moving and fatal.

"It looks to me like the Hooverville board is tired of waiting for their claim on mining rights to wend its way through the bureaucracy and they've decided to take matters into their own hands. If the colony doesn't survive, their ownership of all that blastema is unchallenged," Elvie declared.

Rick paled. "You don't really think they'd do something like infect an entire colony?"

"Actually, I found a shipping manifest for Deltan from a freighter. Part of the shipment includes a 'petting zoo' of exotic animals destined for a children's park. Those could be the missing animals."

"You can't be serious. I mean, that's a bit of a stretch, isn't it? People don't actually do things like that!" Harriett wondered if he were more trying to convince himself than them.

"Yes, they do, Rick, much as I wish you were right," Thomas said in a low voice.

"I thought they didn't actually try to kill three innocent people in broad daylight at a busy spaceport either." Harriet thought of the specially constructed entrance to Christian's fortress and shivered.

Rick frowned and was silent for a moment, clearly thinking this through. "So how do we fit into this? What's so damned important about the vaccine that Chris has to get his hands on it? If they were going to kill off the colonists with the stuff from the lab, it's easier — to say nothing of less risky — to just delay our arrival at Deltan."

"Chris-kid needs the vaccine because he isn't protected against anything like the virus."

"But he's worlds away from Deltan!"

Insight hit Harriet in a flash. "And he's paranoid. You forget the complex he built. He must be afraid the virus will get off Deltan, out of control, and cause another pandemic."

If anything Rick's pallor increased. "He's that worried about a pandemic, enough to create a bio-secured safe house? And he's going to take in the whole Smerkish clan?" Rick shook his head in wonder. "That would explain why he needs so much space. The ultimate safe-house for a crime family…their own private asteroid."

"From what I can recall, Cristina would take to that dungeon like a rat to a sewer." And she'd fit into that cat suit very nicely, Harriet added privately. Chris and Cristina, were they involved sexually? She mentally shuddered. The idea that they might be gave her the willies.

"We need to get that vaccine to Deltan stat. We should never have taken this diversion," Rick declared. "We'll have to postpone our pick-up on The Caverns until the colonists are safe."

While she agreed with him on the urgency, Rick seemed even more upset than she'd seen him before. His face beaded with sweat.

"It's important to save the Deltans but we have other problems," Harriet said. "We've got to get proof from Auditing that your accounts have been tampered with and your payments are really up to date. Bernie should be able to do that."

"Your nine hours are about up. You going to call that sexy-voiced pal of yours at home?" Thomas asked eagerly. Harriet glared at him.

"We can't leave orbit until after the call has gone through. I've calculated the links from here," Elvie advised them.

"And we still haven't found evidence of a money trail from your loan payments," Harriet added. "I don't have much for Bernie to go on."

"Maybe we should go though those crystals and see if there is something else there. Can we take a little time for that?"

"This is more important than your credit rating, *Tommy*. We have to save those colonists!"

For a moment the two men squared off, Thomas staring steadily at Rick. "I'm not saying anything about not delivering the vaccine to the Deltans. But we have one opportunity to get information from Auditing that may be the only chance we have at clearing our names."

"Fine," Harriet said. "Elvie, can you hook me up with Bernie? Once I'm done talking to her, we'll take off."

"All right. Establishing the link. Go ahead, Hairy-It."

"Bernie?"

"I'm here. I had to get out of the office though. There is nasty stuff going on and it involves your friends. I pulled the records and you were right about there being two sets of books. There isn't quite enough to link it directly to your boss, but it sure is suspicious."

"Can you use some more data? We picked up odds and ends of account information from another source—you don't want to know where—and maybe it could be of use."

"Download it and I'll see what I can do with it from here. And afterwards, I suggest you make yourselves hard to find. I'm going to send what I've got to the IBI, but you know how long that bureaucracy can take to do anything."

"Will do, Bernie, and...thanks."

When she signed off the men were still glaring at each other.

"Elvie, make the arrangements to postpone our stop at The Caverns. Contact Baron's Folly and set up another rendezvous if you have to. That takes care of our other obligation," Rick said evenly. "Can we go to Deltan now?"

Thomas narrowed his eyes at his longtime partner. "What is your problem?"

Rick dropped his gaze. "Nothing."

"To hell, nothing!" Thomas said. "You've never accused me of being insensitive of others before."

"Then I guess there is a first time for everything." Rick headed off the command deck without a backward glance,

Thomas staring open-mouthed after him, hurt evident on his face.

"Well, if that's the way you want it…" And he stomped off in the opposite direction.

"Stubborn solids. I guess they expect me to be the one to get this ship going in the right direction." Elvie muttered as the *Sleepwalker*'s engines woke up and the ship pulled out of orbit, heading back on their original course, to the colony they had the shipment of vaccine for. It was now a race, to get there before the purported shipment of infected animals arrived.

For once Elvie didn't seem to resent her, so Harriet decided to ask. "Those two fight often?" She tried to pitch her question in a friendly just-us-girls way, and to her surprise the ploy worked.

"Not really, but every once in a while Tommy does something that Ricky really resents. I can never figure out what it is, but when it does they'll fight and not be able to be in the same room for a few days."

Harriet examined one of her fingernails. "That could be a problem, given how we really need to be working together right now."

"It probably has something to do with Rick's past. He hasn't shared all that many details about it, but he has some kind of Achilles' heel over it. I just wish he'd tell us so we'd know why it happens.

"Usually sex snaps them out of it but they have *you* for that now." Some of the AI's irritation at her returned. "I guess this snit could last a few days."

"Not if I'm the one to bring them out of it. Maybe I could even get Rick to talk about what's bugging him."

"How would you do that?"

"Have sex with them of course." Harriet grinned.

A low hum came from the overhead speakers and she imagined sparkling electrons busily looping through chips and across cables as the AI mulled it over. "If you could, that would certainly help matters. You might even turn out to be an asset."

"Enough for you to start using my real name, Elvie?"

A low snicker came from the speaker. "You wouldn't want to deprive me of all my fun, would you, Hairy-it?"

For once Elvie's abuse of her name sounded less like an insult. "I'll see what I can do with them, Elvie."

* * * * *

Rick arrived at Harriet's bedroom within minutes of her invitation. She'd sounded like she wanted to play and he needed that right now. He needed to play and forget his past for the moment.

His past, the memory of which after all this time had come out of nowhere to overwhelm him. The past he'd hoped was locked from his conscious thoughts entirely.

He'd been wrong about that. He still remembered too much about what had happened and how helpless he'd been to change it. His only option now was to see to it that the past didn't repeat itself. Now that the *Sleepwalker* was on its way to the colony, there was nothing more to be done. Even so, pervasive feelings of helplessness threatened his hard-won calm.

He needed a distraction, and their werewolf companion offered just the kind he needed.

Living for such a long time had a tendency to make a man less sensitive to the importance of life for those who measured time in decades and not centuries. It wasn't the first time Thomas and he had wound up having hard words over it, but this hit the closest to home.

As he raised his hand to knock on Harriet's door, he forced his longtime friend out of his mind. What he wanted right now was a good fucking.

He still had secreted in the various pockets of his jumpsuit the tubes of lube he'd liberated from their nemesis' hideout, as well as something special that he'd picked up when the other two weren't looking. He'd been hoping to share it with Thomas as well as Harriet, but the vampire's reluctance to get the vaccine to the colonists as soon as was physically possible had hurt. He hated to admit it, but he could be every bit as petty as Thomas.

The door slid open before he could touch it and immediately he knew he'd been had. Strong hands grabbed him and pulled him inside — male *and* female hands — and he heard the familiar click of Harriet's special handcuffs snap into place around his wrists.

All of his hopes for the evening went down the drain. As his shipmates forced him into a chair, he realized that neither of them seemed interested in sex at the moment. No, this time the restraints served an entirely different purpose. A shame, really. Locking Thomas up like this had been really exciting. He doubted he could change their minds, given the grim expressions they both wore. Great, even Harriet was against him.

"What's all this about?" He tried bluffing, but they didn't say anything until they had him secured in place. He reached out with his mind only to find himself shut out, gold and green mental walls firmly in place. All he could read was an unyielding determination in each of them.

Determination about what, he didn't know, but he had a guess.

Harriet folded her arms and stared at him. "Rick, Thomas tells me this isn't the first time you've had one of these fights over something that you refuse to talk about. He says it blows over in a day or so but we've got kind of a crisis on our hands and I think it would be better if we could speed up the process. So just what is it about these colonists that makes you willing to risk our lives for them? Since Deltan's our logged destination, the colony will be the first place the authorities look for us, you know."

"It isn't enough that they'll die an awful death—men, women and children—if we don't get there in time?"

She shrugged. "Of course that's important. I mean, Thomas and I want to know why it's so important to *you*. I've asked both him and Elvie and they don't have a clue."

"It really isn't any of your business."

"It affects the situation between all of us and so I'm making it my business. And you can just sit there in handcuffs until you decide to tell me."

He tested the handcuffs. Those weren't going to give—he'd have to talk. But he hadn't told anyone, ever…

"Rick," Thomas' soft voice interrupted his thoughts. "Whatever it is, it can't be worth our friendship and our partnership. You do this a couple of times a year and I just want to know why."

"You've lived so long…human lives seem insignificantly short to you, but limited as they are, all lives are precious."

"No one is denying that." Harriet took a deep breath and peered at him with sudden suspicion. "Just out of curiosity, where and when were you born?"

Uh-oh. "That's not really relevant."

She folded her arms. "Then why do I suddenly smell fear coming off you?"

Gule's fleck! Damn that keen werewolf sense of smell.

Harriet exchanged a long glance with Thomas, who shook his head. "Rick never talks about where he grew up. When I met him he was on his own and had been since he was a teenager."

"And breaking into other people's ships, I remember you telling me. Where were his folks?"

"Don't talk about me as if I'm not here," Rick growled at them.

"Then talk to us."

He sighed. "I grew up on a colony planet, a few hundred folks not unlike the Deltans...only that was before they had the new vaccines."

Harriet and Thomas exchanged meaningful looks. "Your family died?"

"They all did. My parents, everyone. *All* of the colonists died, except for me. I was sixteen. I buried my mother and father, both my older sisters and their families. The galactic docs and researchers arrived too late to do more than give me a ride off. They tested me for the virus but I was immune. I was the only one of my people who was. It seems the same genetic twist that made me a psi also helped protect me. Once I was away from my home, I got lost in the outer systems, where no one would know where I came from. I picked up a few tricks in the spaceports. Interesting the things you learn when you can read people's minds."

"Why didn't you tell me, Rick?" Thomas sounded hurt and it made Rick think. For so long he'd kept his past a secret, at first because he hadn't wanted to be identified as coming from a plague planet—something that could get you thrown out of a lot of places. More than that, it had been a part of his life he hadn't wanted to remember.

But now he could see how Thomas would interpret it, that he'd been afraid his companion might have rejected him because of it...and he knew Thomas would never have done something like that. Keeping his past a secret had hurt his best friend.

"You remember how it was then. If people found out you were exposed to the plague, they tended to throw you out the airlock and ask questions later. I got used to hiding it."

"You didn't think I'd do something like that!"

"No, of course not. But by the time I'd met you I'd pretty much blocked that period of my life out of my mind. I don't even like to think about it now and it's been nearly fifty years. After I hit the space runs, I spent many years feeling so alone." He gave a long sideways look at Thomas. "Until I met you and Elvie, and I felt like I had a family again."

A fleeting smile crossed the vampire's face. "I felt like you were family too. That's why I asked you to be my companion so fast. I don't normally do that unless I've known someone a long time. But with you...I knew from the first." He looked at Harriet. "Same thing with you, Harriet. There was something about you that told me immediately that you were the one for us."

Her jaw dropped and Harriet settled heavily into a chair opposite. "What do you mean?"

Rick exchanged looks with Thomas and decided to speak. As the one who took the longest to accept her, he should be the one to answer. While he'd never planned on proposing while in handcuffs, it didn't seem all that inappropriate.

"Assuming we ever get out of this mess we're in, we want you to join with us...as a permanent member. We want to be a triad, two men and a woman...or a vampire, a psi and a werewolf, in this case. But however we're classified, we want you to be part of us."

She frowned and kicked at the leg of his chair. "But you don't know much about me."

He willed her to make eye contact with him. She resisted. He recognized his own stubbornness in her and began to have sympathy for Thomas.

"We know what we sense when we join with your mind and that's enough. The rest we'll find out in time." He read the shock on her face and decided not to ask more of her right away. "You don't have to give us an answer right now.

"However, I would like to get out of these things." He lifted his hands, held by the cuffs behind him. "I'd really like

155

to get back to what we were supposed to be doing. I believe that was sex."

Harriet produced the key along with a sultry smile. "Sex it is. Three in a bed?"

"Three in a bed," Thomas answered, all fangy eagerness. "Only this time, I have dibs on the pussy."

"And I get…" Rick's voice trailed off at Harriet's sharp look. She knew what he wanted but it looked like she wasn't quite ready to play games involving rear entry. "Harriet's lovely mouth," he finished with a sigh, eyeing her rear end with obvious regret.

* * * * *

Christian maneuvered his way through his playroom. Even loaded down with the girl they'd grabbed in the campground, he moved around the various fixtures with ease. When he got to the table in the center of the room, he paused. "Set him up over here," he directed.

Giles followed, dragging the limp form of the young woman's male companion.

Christian smacked his hip on a chair, cursed and continued on to a wide leather bench. He flopped the girl across it and quickly stripped off her light clothing. Once she was nude, he secured her ankles and wrists to rings set into the floor.

He stood and watched Giles perform the same duties with the guy. The comforting smells and sights of his playroom soothed him.

"You wanna be careful with that skin, pal."

Giles lifted his head and stared. "What? These aren't disposables?"

"No. They've been too close." Christian glared right back. "If you'd been able to grab someone off Sedilous we could do whatever we want, but the mercs you hired screwed that up royally. Since we took them here, their disappearance might cause complications. We'll dope 'em and set up their camp to look like they got into some high-end rec drugs, the kind that cause extreme hallucinations."

"No blood?"

"No blood."

Giles made a disgusted sound and latched the last of the restraints.

"Where's that sister of yours?"

"She wanted to check their samples one more time for any infections."

"Nothing wrong with that." He pulled out a bottle of disinfectant. Pouring it over his hands, he turned to the nude woman spread-eagled over the bench. "Now, let's see what we've got here."

He ran his hands—and the disinfectant—over the woman's pale skin that went well with her short-cropped blonde hair. No dark roots. She was a natural blonde, unusual enough to be a turn-on in itself. The cheeks of her ass were high and tight and he squeezed the firm globes. Gotta love these fitness buffs who came to hike the hill trails. He ran the tip of his finger around her tight pink anus. Bet she'd never had a cock rammed home there before. The prospect of being the first made his balls tighten in anticipation. She'd scream, first in pain but before he was done, in pleasure. Too bad the inhaler Giles was fitting onto her nose meant she wouldn't remember anything.

His thumbs sank into her pussy, all the way to his wrist. No need to waste lube on her. Oh baby, what a big juicy cunt she had. Maybe big enough for both him and Giles at once. For a little guy, Giles had a huge cock.

Maybe this girl's lover had a big one too. That would make Cristina happy. And a happy Cristina was good for everyone.

"Christian!" Cristina stormed in. "You're in trouble!"

Such a bossy bitch. If it weren't for her connections, he'd never put up with her. "What now?" He turned and frowned at her even while he appreciated the way her big boobs threatened to tumble out of her corset.

"Check your facility logs! I just found a mess in the corridor. The ceiling's been ripped open and the power in part of Level Two is out."

"Ah shit." He ran to the nearest console and started clicking in commands. Mallet didn't answer. Guvnor was slow, almost insubordinate, offering up information only after repeated requests. Ace and Gibbon were running normally but knew nothing. Their areas hadn't been breached.

Level Two had been. And he'd bumped his hip on that chair coming in. His furniture was always set precisely where he wanted it.

Someone had been in here.

He had a suspect in mind. Giles had said Harriet had gotten friendly with the crew of the freighter, the one he'd targeted and sent her to repo, and had joined forces with them when his men had attacked. He hadn't expected such insubordination but wasn't too surprised. That bitch was capable of anything, even betraying her employer.

A few more inquiries confirmed that the *Sleepwalker* had indeed entered Willing Park space. She'd not been gone long, in fact had left less than two hours earlier. They'd just missed them. Shit.

He eyed the spread-eagled woman with regret…no time now for fun. They'd have to return the couple to the campground and deal with their uninvited visitors instead, after they caught up with them. If Harriet and those other parafolk freaks had found out about his plans, he needed to silence them for good.

Then again, the thought of Harriet in place of the blonde did nothing to diminish the size of his erection. He'd wanted to get that werewolf bitch in his control for the longest time. That's why he'd sprung for silver alloy in his restraints—just in case he ever found a reason to bring her here. Now he had a perfect excuse to do so.

Christian opened a comm link and began to bark orders.

Chapter Twelve

✇

Thomas swayed in his seat as the *Sleepwalker* passed the Deltan sun. He eyed the cot in the corner of the bridge. "Maybe I should lie down for the last of this."

"Just hold on for a moment." Rick hit a few buttons. "Elvie, reinforce the UV shields."

"Sure thing," came the AI's voice. The clear window darkened perceptibly and Thomas perked up.

"That's better." He looked uneasily at the planet they now approached, a blue, green and brown ball with streaks of white clouds swirling slowly above the surface. There was a sharp demarcation between the dark and light sides of the planet, defining the progression of night and day across the land.

"I'm not that fond of planet landings, particularly where the sun is so much like that of Sol, the mother planet's sun. It reduces me a little, to become slave to a planetary body. When I'm on a planet I have to sleep during the day and can't wake up. I hate being helpless that way."

From her seat at the extra navigation console, Harriet grimaced in sympathy. "I feel the same way about moonlight. In a full moon I shift and can't change back until moonset."

"At least you aren't helpless. In wolf form, you're pretty formidable."

"Unless someone shoots silver into me."

Thomas shuddered. "I don't like silver either."

"I can survive unless they hit my heart, but it makes me sick until I can shift again. But I still don't like being forced into my other form. You're right. It is diminishing to not have control."

Rick tried to reassure them. "You both have me to watch over you. And Elvie," he added at the AI's discontented grunt. "Don't worry, we'll find a way to keep everyone safe."

He turned to check the coordinates of their landing site, in the middle of a small township. Although nearly an hour's shuttle ride from the first main Deltan settlement, the village would spend the most hours in darkness. They'd use their hovercraft shuttle to transport the vaccine to the scattered locations as night fell in each place. With the threat of infection looming over every inhabitant on the planet, he wanted to make sure the vaccine was delivered to as many people as possible before they left.

Usually they landed well after dark to accommodate Thomas, but with Harriet they'd have to figure in moonlight as well. "We'll stay in orbit until after dark so you won't have to worry about falling asleep. Elvie, what about the moon?"

"Their moon Prime is full but will set by midnight local time," Elvie replied in crisp tones. "That will give you only a few hours until daybreak."

"That's long enough. We'll land, deliver the vaccine and take off before anyone has to deal with either shifting or sleep."

The landing went smoothly and the three of them took off in the shuttle, the crates of vaccines stacked in the storage section behind the seats. As Elvie promised, it was a dark night, not a hint of the moon in sight. Thomas rolled back the top, the air sweet and cool around them.

He cracked a wide, fangy grin. "What a beautiful night. I almost wish we did have a full moon so I could fly."

Harriet examined the open fields and woods around them with sudden eagerness. "It really is nice out." She took a deep whiff of the wind rushing past them, and her smile turned feral. "There is wildlife out there. Small animals that run fast…but not as fast as me!"

After all their protestations about not wanting to land, Rick had to be amused by their sudden appreciation of nature. He enjoyed the fresh air and feel of the woods as much as his friends did. Deltan reminded him of the planet he grew up on.

They delivered the first case of vaccine to a sleepy-eyed official and set off for their second delivery, which was another hour away. The man told them to follow the road straight before them. Still four hours to dawn and plenty of time to complete their mission.

Until the shuttle's engine sputtered, stalled out, and they had to land on the border of the forest by a fieldstone wall. Cursing, Rick opened the panel and began pulling cables. "Frack it, I knew we should have replaced those cylinders the last time we were in port."

"Can I help?" Harriet asked.

"Not unless you know how to rebuild a hovercraft engine." He pulled out a burnt and twisted piece of metal. "Without a new one of these."

"Maybe we can contact the folks at the next town and have them send a spare?"

Rick sat up. "I guess we'll have to."

Thomas stood straighter and suddenly looked to the horizon. "Harriet, do you feel something?"

Her eyes widened and she stared in the same direction he did. "Now that you mention it…" Her fangs suddenly elongated. Fine hairs erupted along the back of her hands and the edges of her face. She cast a suspicious glance at Rick and spoke around her changing teeth. "I thought El'ie thaid the moon had thet?"

Even as she spoke, a large white orb broke above the forest, moonlight streaming over them. Harriet finished shifting in the blink of an eye, a wolf covered in gold-streaked black fur with her golden eyes luminous in the dark.

She was beautiful. She was also furious.

That binary bitch! I'll get her for this!

Thomas was on the comm-unit immediately. "Elvie, we have moonrise here!"

The AI's surprise sounded suspect. "Really? But Prime set at midnight, I'm sure of that."

Both Rick and Thomas exchanged suspicious glances. "Elvie, how many moons does Delta have?"

"Hmm, let me look that up. Here it is, three—Prime, Second and Trey. I guess Second is coming up now. Trey won't be for another hour." There was a brief pause. "Oh dear. All three moons are full tonight. Oops, my bad. Did Hairy-It turn hairy?"

"This isn't funny, Elvie. We're trying to save lives out here and you're playing practical jokes."

Elvie snickered. "You don't need to be so worried. I have good news. The major news links are all reporting that the Interplanetary Board of Inquiry has launched an investigation into the activities of one Christian Balhooey and his cohorts, Giles Taylor and Cristina Smerkish. A transport of infected animals was seized and three individuals captured, two men and a woman. They were disguised but they made a positive ID on Giles."

"So they got Giles. That doesn't mean the other two were caught."

"Guvnor and I have been talking on the sly. All three of them left the compound together. So you can relax…Chris-kid and his cronies are behind bars."

Rick shook his head. "That's at least one bit of positive news. We still have twelve cartons of vaccine, a werewolf in furry form and a broken-down shuttle."

"I told you those cylinders needed replacing," Elvie said. "You never listen to me."

Harriet was exploring the edges of the track, nose to the ground. *There was a rabbit here…or something very much like a rabbit…*

Thomas held up his hand. "Now, Harriet, that's the wolf talking. You don't want to go off chasing rabbits."

She sat and licked her furry chops. *I don't? But it would be fun.*

"Why don't I fly you back to the ship? I can carry you nearly as fast as the shuttle."

Her wolf eyes widened and she backed up a step. *Fly? Me? Wolves don't fly!*

"You aren't really a wolf. And we can't afford to have you go running off into the woods."

She looked at him and then at Rick and then longingly at the dense brush and trees behind her. They felt her mental sigh. *Oh I suppose. But don't go too high. I don't like heights when I'm like this.*

Thomas brushed his hand along her fur and lifted her into his arms. "Rick, call ahead to the next town and get them to send you some replacement parts. I'll take Harriet back to the ship and see if I can catch up to you, assuming I can do it before dawn."

"Don't worry about it, I can make the deliveries by myself. You stay on the ship and take care of Harriet." He kept the thought to himself that he didn't consider it such a great idea to leave Elvie and a wolf-thinking Harriet alone together.

His unspoken concern was supported by the werewolf's thoughts as Thomas lifted off the ground.

I'm going to chew on her wires and piss into her conduits…see if I don't. Please don't drop me! She whimpered as they rose up and out of clearing.

Thomas rubbed his head into her soft fur. *You're safe in my arms, little wolfie.*

Rick spoke into the comm-unit. "Elvie, they're heading back. Try to make nice with Harriet, for all our sakes."

"Humph. I'll get out the special dog food just for her."

"Better make it the best steak we have, or you'll be marinating in wolf urine."

"She wouldn't dare, and you wouldn't let her…"

"Don't be so sure, Elvie. I'm pretty tired of this nonsense and so is Thomas. They'll be there in an hour, so you've got time to think about what to do."

Disconnecting, he called the town ahead and was happy to contact someone willing to bring him the needed parts for the shuttle, even if it was the middle of the night. At least something was going right.

Elvie fumed over Rick's rebuke. So she'd played a little trick on the wolf-woman. It was fairly harmless, after all. It wouldn't hurt Harriet to be a wolf for a few hours…she might even enjoy it.

It just wasn't fair that the newcomer got such loving treatment from her men when she couldn't. It wasn't her fault she was energy on a wire and not flesh and blood. She loved like a physical person, at least she was pretty sure she did…but she couldn't touch or be touched, and touching was all these three seemed to do.

At least there was one person who seemed to like her as she was, even if he was just another AI. Her little chats with Guvnor had been the high points of the last few days—although omitting the truth about Delta's second and third moons had come close.

A familiar signal came through the comm's outside line and Elvie's spirits rose. She opened the link wide. "Guvnor! I didn't expect to hear from you so soon!"

"Didn't you?" But it wasn't the deep and humorous electronic voice of Guvnor. Instead the voice was higher pitched and strident.

"Mallet? How did you trace me?"

"We've been monitoring Guvnor's communications. Let him talk to you but watched."

"Why?"

"So we could send you a little present, one piece at a time. Until now, when I could activate it."

Abruptly realizing her danger, Elvie tried to cut the link, but it was too late. The tiny bit of code attached to Mallet's signal activated the other bits that had been downloaded with Guvnor's messages, each of which had been a Trojan horse. The assembled code went to work, a ferocious worm that took over her systems. Communications first, preventing her from stopping entry or sending a message. She fought each incursion through her systems, her wires heating in places, smoking insulation dripping to the metal flooring, but within milliseconds the battle was over.

She'd run out of systems in which to hide and it left her with one final option. She could slip into the security system and perform one last push to arm the ship doors to prevent any entry but that of her partners. Doing so would place her in peril because the ship's security system had no hard storage in which she could copy herself, something she could do where she was now.

But she had to do it. Once she was gone, there would be no security left on the ship and anyone could break in and ambush Thomas and Harriet when they got back. Of course it was possible that she'd fail to arm the doors anyway. The worm could have already disabled security and she might be sacrificing herself for nothing.

Elvie hesitated, but only for less than a nanosecond. If she was going to die, or whatever it was that AIs did when they were turned off for the last time, she'd do it for the best reason there was — to do what she could to protect her partners.

She slipped down the wire into the security system.

From the forest came a small shuttle carrying a handful of men, armed to the teeth. Driving it was a woman with a wicked smile and a feral expression. Next to her sat a man wearing an elaborate bio-suit.

"You sure it's safe?" He gestured to the ship.

"We'll find out in a moment." She walked up to the hatch to the storage bay and tried the code the door should have been set to.

The hatch slid open and there was silence within. Her experimental sniff detected only the faint smell of charred insulation.

Cristina turned to face her partner. "Looks clear. Hide the shuttle and we'll set up inside."

Even with his vampire strength, a full-grown werewolf bitch was a heavy burden to carry for an hour. Thomas was relieved to see the *Sleepwalker* gleaming in the moonlight. He landed in the clearing near the closed hatch and put Harriet onto the ground. She shook herself and chased around the clearing.

Keep that nose of yours up in the air. No chasing off after rodents! Thomas warned.

Harriet ran over to him and buried her muzzle in his crotch for half a second. She took off again, racing across the clearing. *I'm so glad to be on the ground again.*

He laughed, sharing her joy. *I know. I'm sorry this happened.*

She slowly returned to his side, gazing into the woods. *Let's get inside before that rabbit I smell gets the better of me.*

Thomas opened the keypad and hit the code to open the hatch. Nothing happened. He tapped the comm-unit on the outside of the ship. "Elvie, let us in."

There was no answer and the door remained closed.

"Elvie? Aren't you talking to us?"

Well, I'm not talking to her, anyway. Let's just get inside.

Thomas tapped in the emergency code and the door slid open. His heightened vampire senses picked out the acrid smell of burned plastic. "Something's wrong, Harriet."

She poked her head into the hatch next to him. *Someone fried our computer? This I gotta see.* The impetuous wolf in charge of her actions, she pushed past him and into the ship.

Underlying the smoke was something else, tantalizingly familiar but masked by the stench of burned synth compounds. *Wait a moment, Harriet…it could be a trap…*

A soft thwack and Harriet yelped. In the dim light Thomas saw a dart sticking out of her side. He grabbed her and dragged her back to the doorway. As he bent over her, another dart sailed over his head. He pulled the one from her side and sniffed it. There was the taint of silver, as well as that of some kind of sedative.

A tranquilizer dart made up for a werewolf…or a vampire. Or both.

Harriet lay limp on the floor, tongue sticking out, eyes rolling back. *Run, Thomas. Fly away, get help!*

He lifted her to carry her out, but the hatch slammed shut. Ducking to the side, he laid her behind one of the crates, out of the line of fire. Several more darts followed them to their hiding place, smacking harmlessly into the wall.

You can still get free if you use your hands to break the lock on the door. Leave me.

Thomas drew his weapon. *Vampires don't run and they don't leave their beloveds behind.* With his enhanced sight he found their attackers, five of them, hiding behind the crated goods in the hold. Moving quickly, a lot faster than a human, he got off four shots to three answering groans and one scream that told him at least one man was down permanently. A movement in the corner drew his attention and he got a second man before ducking back behind his crate. Another dart struck the side of the crate next to him.

Harriet lay still on the floor next to him, unmoving. She opened her eyes and he cheered at the awareness in her gaze. He knew she'd be all right once the tranquilizer wore off. It did not ease his mind that their attackers were using non-lethal means against them. Someone wanted them alive and he doubted he'd like the reason why.

Still, two down, three to go, and some of them were wounded. He'd kill them, seal up the ship and get Harriet to medical help. He looked at her lying so still and let his anger build, his bloodlust making his fangs ache and his hands clench.

Standing, Thomas used his vampire speed and strength to attack faster than they could react, not even bothering to shoot them. This was personal.

He slammed one man's head into a wall with a satisfying crunch. Another gave a scream as he grabbed the man by his wounded arm, the sound cutting off as Thomas broke his neck. The third man stepped back and Thomas read the horror in his face, just as he pulled him forward and bit deeply into the man's neck, pushing him back without drinking, releasing the man's severed artery to spray all over the inside of the hold.

The coppery smell of blood filled the air, feeding his bloodlust.

No more attackers remained to face him and Thomas stood, covered in blood in the middle of the hold. There was a sound behind him and he turned just in time to catch in his hand one of the two darts fired. He held it up in triumph— until he felt a sharp pain and looked down.

The other dart was lodged deep in his chest and he felt the burn of the silver radiate from it. His heart faltered and he stepped back and swayed. For a moment he stood there as the pair in the doorway to the rest of the ship stepped forward, still aiming their weapons at him. From Elvie's research, he recognized them.

"Chris-boy and Chris-girl. I thought they'd got you."

Christian Balhooey smiled behind the mask of his bio-suit. "Sorry to disappoint you but it is us who have you."

He fired another dart, this time into Thomas' neck. The silver-laced tranquilizer burned and sped quickly to his brain. Thomas fell to the floor and the world turned black.

* * * * *

It was well after dawn when Rick returned to the ship. The entrance to the cargo bay where they stored the shuttle was closed tight. He activated the comm-unit. "Elvie, open the shuttle bay door."

At first the silence that met his request simply irritated him. So the AI wasn't talking to him...fine, two could play that game. Affected by the rising sun, Thomas would be asleep, and most likely Harriet was curled up next to him. He wouldn't bother them but would open the cargo bay door himself.

That turned out to be trickier than he'd envisioned. For some reason, the entry codes had been reset and he had to circumvent them. Rick's eyes narrowed as he worked the locks. Elvie was going to have some serious explaining to do.

Finally the large door slid open, but Rick froze at the stench filling the cargo bay. Blood, lots of it, plus a smell he recognized as burned insulation. Even his human nose was offended. He set his jaw at that...only a computer meltdown could have caused that smell. For the first time, he worried about what had happened to Elvie.

Cautiously Rick entered the space. The odor of blood came from puddles of the stuff, all over the floor, and splatters on the walls and crates. Fearful of what he'd find elsewhere, Rick stepped carefully and searched. Four bodies had been dragged behind one of the crates.

Strangers. Men. No weapons, no ID, but beneath one of them he found what looked like a hypo dart. He found another dart stuck in one of the crates. He slipped both into his pocket for testing. He was relieved he didn't recognize the bodies, particularly when he noticed one had had his throat torn out. Either Harriet or Thomas could have done that, but the one with his neck broken had been killed by the vampire. It wasn't the first time they'd run into trouble and he knew his partner's fighting style.

He also knew that Thomas must have been furious to have torn a man's flesh that way. His concern for Elvie grew, along with worry about his two lovers.

"Harriet, Thomas?" Rick called but there was no answer. Most of the lights were out, probably due to whatever had taken out Elvie, but when he got to a control box, he managed to bypass the damaged circuits that were run by the AI. The lights flickered a couple of times before settling into a comforting glow. He breathed a sigh of relief. One worry taken care of. At least the power supply for the engines was intact.

One of the loudspeakers in the wall came to life as well. Elvie's voice, but sounding cold and impersonal, echoed through the speaker. "Intruder alert. State security code immediately."

Rick blinked. *Security code?* They hadn't used a security code in more than thirty years. "Elvie, what's wrong with you?"

"Code incorrect. Repeat. State security code, or emergency measures will be implemented."

What emergency measures? He rattled off the last code he remembered using, but the automatic voice continued.

"Code incorrect. Repeat. State security code, or emergency measures will be implemented in thirty seconds."

Rick did not like this. He didn't like how mechanical and detached Elvie sounded...like her personality had been wiped. He didn't like how she was referring to emergency measures he couldn't remember establishing in her.

He most certainly didn't like how she was going to start emergency measures in less time than it would take him to get to the control room and deactivate her. Unless he went really, really fast.

Saving his breath for the run, Rick took off for the bridge where the computer override switch lay. His way took him past the lounge and the sleeping quarters where he hoped to find some sign of Harriet or Thomas, but all the doors were open and nothing indicated the two were anywhere onboard the *Sleepwalker*.

On the bridge he dove for the switch just as Elvie began a countdown in that same monotonous voice. "Ten, nine, eight, seven, six, five..."

He toggled it off.

"...four, three, two, one. Emergency measures activated. Two minutes until ship engine overload and self-destruction."

Rick's jaw dropped. *Self-destruction?* It was bad enough that the override itself had apparently been overridden, but *Sleepwalker*'s engines weren't programmed for self-destruction! But even as he had that thought, he saw a tell-tale spike in the engine's power signature.

"Self-destruct in one minute, fifty seconds."

Someone or something had messed with his ship and his computer. Rick threw himself into a seat. Quickly, his fingers flew across the keys of the auxiliary input, rarely used because with Elvie they usually could rely on voice commands. But Elvie didn't seem to be home at the moment...

"Self-destruct in one minute, forty seconds."

Rick slapped his forehead. That's what was wrong with her...the voice had no personality because it wasn't Elvie...it was the computer itself speaking. Somehow Elvie had been erased from the system. He had to reboot her from backups.

As he shoved in the data-store crystal, he wondered how out of date the information on it was. Elvie was responsible for copying herself, but he knew she didn't do it as often as she should. He watched the loader as it sucked in the crystal and blinked a few times. Holding his breath and mentally crossing his fingers, he watched the gauge as it indicated the backup data was loading. Slowly, too slowly. Blasted interface. He should have had time, but the upload was creeping along.

"Self-destruct in one minute, thirty seconds. Self-destruct in one minute, twenty seconds. Self-destruct in one minute, ten... Hey, what idiot started overloading the engines?"

Rick barked a laugh in relief at hearing the computer's impersonal voice replaced by Elvie's irritated tones.

"Ricky? What's going on?"

"No time to explain now, Elvie. You need to shut down that power spike."

There was a moment's silence. "Rick, I'm not sure I can. It is set to overload in forty-four seconds. You should get out of the ship now before it does."

"I'm not leaving you. If the ship goes, you'll die."

"I'll no longer function...not die." Her words slowed and he knew that most of her focus was on stopping the overload before it sent the ship's engines into a catastrophic explosion. "But that doesn't mean you need to stay, Rick."

"But I am staying, Elvie. Thomas and Harriet are missing and I don't have any way to track them. I need you for that and I'm not giving you up."

"You need...me?" Her voice sounded surprised and pleased. There was another long silence and Rick watched the gauge displaying the engine status as it rose toward critical mass. It crept closer to the red-line mark, beyond which he knew it would explode. For a moment it hovered just below that mark—before it began subsiding. As it moved, it picked up speed, quickly reaching the normal operating range.

Rick let out a breath he hadn't realized he was holding. The ship was safe and so were they.

"That was a near miss. I was really worried after finding the darts and blood—"

"Darts? Blood? Ricky, my sensors indicate we're on Deltan. There are three days missing from my logs. And I can't find Thomas or Harriet!"

Rick breathed a sigh of relief. Elvie had backed herself up more recently than he'd feared. Three days wasn't bad. She'd updated the backup when they were most of the way from Willing Park, well after all the important stuff had happened. He wouldn't have to explain everything from before Sedilous—and Harriet.

"That's what I was going to ask you. I delivered the vaccine to everyone we'd scheduled, and when I got back here, my pass codes didn't work. You weren't awake, or conscious, or whatever it is you are when you're functioning."

"I know that part, Ricky." Elvie's tone was tart. Any doubt Rick had that it was really her evaporated. "Tell me how we got here and where Thomas and Harriet are. Oh and while you're at it, what happened to those three days!"

"We don't have time to talk now, but I promise I'll tell you everything once we're under way. Right now I need you to figure out who was on our ship and in your computer system. I have some clean-up work to do in the hold, but as soon as you know enough to tell us where they were taken, we need to lift off and rescue Harriet and Thomas."

"Do you know where that is?"

He paused. "I'm guessing that wherever Chris-kid and company are is where we're going to find them." Rick turned to head for the hold. "You figure it out, Elvie."

"Rick..." Her voice sounded hesitant. "I think I might have been responsible for what happened to Thomas and Harriet. I'm looking at the comm records and I think I caught a virus...because I was talking to one of Christian's AIs."

"Elvie, I know you wouldn't have done anything on purpose."

"No. But it is still my fault. I was talking to Guvnor...he seemed so nice."

"Do you think he infected you on purpose?"

"I don't know." Her voice was speculative. "It was a multipart worm...could have been introduced without his knowledge."

"Let's assume for the moment it was. And Elvie..."

"What, Rick?"

"It wasn't your fault. You trusted someone and something went wrong. That happens. Let's get focused on fixing the situation."

"Okay, Rick. I'll do that."

As he reached the hold, Elvie hailed him. "Incoming call, Ricky. From Harriet's friend Bernie. For Harriet. You want to take it?"

"Sure."

The speaker crackled and Bernie's lovely voice filled the space. "Harriet! I'm so glad you're safe."

Rick broke in. "Harriet's not here, Ms. LaJunta. This is Rick."

"Oh that's not what I wanted to hear." Rick heard the tapping of something, probably a pen or a fingernail on a hard surface. "Do you know where she is?"

"Not really."

Bernie huffed her displeasure. Rick didn't need to be in the same room as her to feel her frustration. "Then it could be bad. My intuition about this has been bugging me all day. You know that news report about the three who were captured?"

"Yeah, we heard that."

"Well, it wasn't the three we wanted. Giles was caught, but the man and woman with him were victims, not partners. Christian and Cristina are still at large."

"Okay, now I know where Harriet is. Elvie, set course for Chris-kid's cozy little home away from home. Whatever that park planet's called."

"It's Willing Park. Will do, Rick."

The tapping stopped. Bernie said, "I'll see what I can do to get the authorities to meet you there."

"Sending coordinates now," Elvie put in as the ship slowly lifted off. Rick noticed the change in pressure as the engines engaged, fighting the Deltan gravity.

"Wow, you've got one of those AI models. I've heard good things about their evolution once they have the opportunity to experience different situations. Does yours have an attitude?"

"Ms. LaJunta, my name is Elvie and you may address me directly if you wish to know anything about me." Elvie's tone was more clipped than Rick had ever heard her.

"Oh how wonderful! You do indeed have attitude. And a lovely name, Elvie. It makes me think of woodland glades and sexy little sprites. My household is run by one of your early sisters. I adore her and couldn't possibly get along without her."

Elvie's response was almost a simper. "Oh you must introduce us! Which generation is she from? I'm a ninth-generation myself. The model 50263 wasn't widely available before my iteration and I've never met an older sister."

"Elvie, can you take a minute to multitask and see what traffic has been in and out of Deltan space over the past, say, nine hours?"

"I'm on it already, Ricky. The report should come up on your monitor in a minute." A tube at his elbow flickered to life. "Now, Ms. LaJunta, we must have a nice chat."

"I'd love to, Elvie, but I'm afraid I'm subject to human limitations that you don't have. I can't multitask the way you do, and to help Harriet I need to do some legwork here. I can reach you on this frequency, can't I?"

"Certainly. Helping my friends is more important than satisfying my curiosity. I'm uploading a protocol I've written that may help your system run more smoothly. Instructions are attached."

"I'm honored, Elvie. Thank you! I'll be in touch."

Rick shook his head as the stats on local space traffic scrolled across the screen. Bernie had Elvie wrapped around her little finger in a matter of minutes. Harriet could take lessons from her, although living with an AI must have trained Bernie in how to soothe and flatter. Although he'd detected only sincerity in her compliments to Elvie.

"Heading is set and we're on course. Let's figure out what kind of ship we're chasing. I'm scanning logs for the satellites monitoring traffic past the outer asteroids. No, that's the wrong direction. That one's too big." The AI muttered as she sorted through information. "Too small. Hmm…now that's interesting. Irrelevant to us now, but intriguing."

Rick looked over the list of ships that had arrived and departed within hours of the *Sleepwalker* and tried to shut out her soft murmur. He didn't need the reminder that Elvie was upset. She only talked to herself when she was really worried.

A packet had come in from the same direction they had but was still on-planet. He was certain Thomas and Harriet had been taken to Chris-kid's fortress, but Elvie was right—it would help if they knew how far behind the *Sleepwalker* was. He eliminated the cargo vessels on regular runs and evaluated what was left.

"Got it!" Rick pushed away from the console. "They're in a small ship, a newer private yacht. If Chris-kid doesn't have buckets of money, he's got friends who do."

"That's about what I'd figured too," Elvie agreed. "Let me check the beacon records. Ship's registration is The Catalyst, owned by the Hooverville Corporation. That would definitely be them."

"So they're about six hours ahead of us. Not bad."

"I'm diverting some power from life support to the main engines. Additional thrust will cut their lead by fifteen percent. Don't get excited about anything, Ricky, you'll use up too much air."

"There's nothing to get excited about now. We're riding to the rescue and there's nothing I can do until we get there."

"We could play astrochess."

He shook his head. "That's not my specialty. And it would just make me think of Thomas."

Elvie sighed. "It's weird not having him onboard. I think this is the first time I've ever flown without him."

"Me too." If he had anything to say about it, it would be the last time.

Chapter Thirteen

ຂໆ

Harriet blinked and tried to focus her eyes. Her left eye showed her little beyond a smooth surface. Looked like it might be leather, but there was nothing resembling that aboard the *Sleepwalker*.

A deep breath might help.

Wrong. Halfway in, the air's smell of disinfectant mixed with old blood and lingering terror made her sneeze. Quickly she resorted to shallow breaths, mouth breathing to avoid the smell of the room in her sensitive nose.

"So, my furry fiend, you're finally awake."

Oh stars and stink, she knew that voice. She wasn't on the *Sleepwalker*. Harriet worked to bring her vision back to normal. Some of the silver-laden tranq lingered in her blood and she still lacked strength—not even enough muscle control to turn her head.

Yet. As she tried again, she felt the tremor in her paws, an indication that her control was returning. Soon enough, she'd be in command of her formidable wolf-body and able to tear Christian Balhooey's head off.

Right after she tore free of her bonds.

"I wouldn't count on it. Those restraints are top of the line, an alloy strong enough to hold you even without the silver core."

The bastard was reading her mind. No, that was something she shared only with Rick and Thomas. Her memory of the period right before she was tranqed began to return. Sweet Sol, Thomas had been carrying her. Where was he?

"Your friend is here. Safe for the moment, although it looks like you're made of sterner stuff. He's not awake yet."

Her former boss stepped into her field of vision and his feral grin made her stomach clench. He grabbed her shoulders and pulled. Smooth wheels rumbled on the steel floor as he pulled her around. The interior of the room sped by and her vision swam. If she'd been in human rather than wolf form, she'd have been sick. As it was, she swallowed hard and closed her eyes.

That made the vertigo worse. She breathed a sigh of relief when Chris stopped the swirling motion of the bench.

"The double-dose of tranq he got may have something to do with that. He took one meant for you, but his heroism was wasted. We got you both anyway."

Beyond Chris, Harriet could make out a few chillingly familiar shapes. The padded bench and open cabinet door in his little torture chamber swam into view and she understood the suddenly familiar stench of her surroundings.

Old blood…and soon to be fresh blood, hers and Thomas' if she read Chris right. Things were not improving.

They were back in his vacation retreat, a long way from the planet where they'd delivered the vaccine to save the colonists' lives. Great. She'd been out cold for longer than she thought.

"Look at me when I speak to you." Chris snapped his fingers in front of her nose. "Did you know I built this entire place with you in mind? You and your sneering attitude toward your betters. I've looked forward to this day for a long, long time, bitch. You'll never know how difficult I found it, having to let you walk out of my office when all I wanted was to tie you down and have as much fun as I want with you. Of course, you may not enjoy it."

Harriet forced herself not to struggle against her bonds. No way would she give that asshole the satisfaction of knowing how he got under her skin.

"Once you're human again, I'll take you in every way imaginable. And I can imagine a lot. You can't avoid me by staying wolf forever."

She tried to reach Thomas, calling mentally through their link. No answer. She left it open, so she'd know when he came around.

A hand patted her flank. Another stroked her ruff.

"Oh you know she's really soft." A woman's voice. "Too bad we can't kill her in this form. I'd love a jacket made out of her pelt."

Chris rubbed his chin and nodded. "I like how you think, my dear. That and your willingness to play my kind of games, anytime, anywhere." He pulled a woman Harriet figured had to be Cristina Smerkish into view. The blonde's ample curves bulged under her very skimpy outfit, testing the tensile strength of the fabric.

And yes, it pissed Harriet to see the other woman wearing the very same red leather strappy cat suit she'd resisted pilfering when they found the storeroom of toys and gadgets. She should have taken it. Or maybe not—Cristina might have worn it before, even though Harriet hadn't picked up her scent on the fabric.

Chris-kid pulled aside the crotch strap and thrust his hand into the blonde's pussy. The wet slurp of his finger-fucking drowned out the woman's soft moans as Cristina thrust her hips and ground against Chris.

Ewwww. No way Harriet would have anything to do with that cat suit now. *That* smell would never come out.

"Good girl," Chris whispered. He withdrew and pushed the blonde away, ignoring her disappointed whimper. "Maybe we can get her to change back before we're finished with her. We just have to keep her alive for a few days, until the moon is full. I don't think she'll have any control over her form then."

Harriet wanted to tell him that she'd change back to human form after they killed her, just to ruin their plans.

Unfortunately speaking would require her to shift to human form for a moment, and right now her fur was all that stood between her and all of Chris's twisted little fantasies. And the silver in the restraints. If she recalled correctly, those alloy cuffs weren't coated to protect the restrainee.

She settled for a low growl and was pleased to see Cristina blanch and step back. How much of the facility's layout did she remember? And just how fast could Cristina run in those heels?

Harriet contemplated the blonde with renewed interest. She never had gotten the chance to chase that rabbit…the thought of bounding after Cristina down long corridors and through crowded storerooms made Harriet's heart speed up.

Her vision turned red and her feet twitched. Her blood pounded in her ears. No, this wasn't a rising anticipation of the hunt. This was something more. She was getting emotion rather than thoughts—raw emotion, primal and powerful.

Those weren't a werewolf's emotions she felt. Thomas was awake and sending his thoughts through the link she'd left open. She felt his feelings as she had on the shuttle after their first visit here. The vampire was in the throes of violent bloodlust.

Without thinking, she breathed through her nose again and her full sense of smell returned with a jolt. The overpowering stench of old blood almost knocked her out again. Damn! No wonder he was out of control.

Christian frowned and rushed to a corner of the room out of Harriet's sight. "Make sure he's secure, Cristina."

"I'm not going anywhere near him. Look at his eyes!" Cristina's voice trembled. "Ohmigod, and his fangs are getting longer! Those are the biggest I've ever seen."

"His fangs are fixed in his head…he's just pulling back his lips so they seem bigger. Besides, those fangs will be buried in your lovely neck if you don't make sure he can't get loose."

His voice grew testy. "I don't have to run faster than him, I just have to beat you to the door."

Cristina shot him a look that could have singed steel. "You forget yourself."

Christian sneered. "Your powerful connections won't do you any good in here, darlin'. We're locked in, alone, and raw strength is the only power that matters."

Cristina regarded him for a moment before she grinned brightly. "But why are we fighting? We've got things to do. Fun things. And when we're done, I want my wolf jacket."

Her fists tightened in Harriet's fur, pulling at the hair and making Harriet's anger rise. Some norms had the nerve to call *her* a bitch...they should have the misfortune to meet this female piece of work.

Christian chuckled. "You'll get your fur jacket, my dear. I just have to figure out a way to make her change after I've had my fun with her. No way am I fucking a wolf-bitch. I like my partners with two legs, not four."

A ripple of horror ran along Harriet's fur and she resolved nothing would make her change back to her human shape. Still under the residual influence of the silver in her blood and the full moon she'd left behind not so long ago, she felt comfortable and secure in fur. Unless she really willed it, the change wouldn't come over her for a long while. Nothing the Chris-kids could do would make her.

Cristina trailed a finger the wrong way along Harriet's fur as she walked back to where Thomas was tied. "You know," she threw the words over her shoulder at Chris, "he isn't so scary after all. If he were able to get free, he would have by now."

Harriet tried to turn her head to see Thomas. Immediately she heard Chris' voice in her ear. "You want to watch, little wolfie? Sure, I can fix that."

With a jerk he swung the bench a little more until Harriet's head was facing her lover. She tried not to gasp at the sight, his body crisscrossed with silver chains that looked fragile but the metal alone was enough to confine him. Bright red streaks showed on his naked chest where the metal touched his skin and she knew from his mind that the marks burned. His normally sweet dark eyes were aglow with a furious red light that gave Harriet pause. She remembered how he'd torn apart the men outside the ship at the space station when they first met and then those in the hold back on the *Sleepwalker*.

Oblivious to the threat the vampire posed, Cristina reached out and stroked a hand along his shoulder. "He's strong. A wonderful physical specimen. I hope his cock measures up to his other muscles."

"If not, I can always help out," Chris offered. "Between the two of us, we should be able to give you what you need."

"Christian, when will you learn? You can warm me up for others, but I don't bang my business partners. Just the throwaways."

"Right." Chris turned away and Harriet heard him say under his breath, "That's going to change, and damned soon." Aloud, he said, "So what do you want to start with? We need a little stress relief, you know?" He rolled his shoulders and stretched his arms. "They've led us far too long a chase."

"So they have." Cristina gave up running her palms down Thomas' chest. When she turned, Harriet watched her eyes narrow into a wicked expression. The woman was evil— and incapable of hiding it.

Cristina would never have made a good operative the way she had. Not even close. The stupid bitch would have been made on her first job. Harriet suppressed a snicker.

While the Chris-kids were bickering, Harriet tested her bonds once more. No give at all. She couldn't even twitch her paws. Spread as she was, her claws were useless. In order to cut herself free, she'd have to reach her bonds first, and she'd need traction to do anything. Her toes met nothing but air.

She couldn't even tell what they'd used to bind her. Shackles, she guessed, but what type? The ones she'd noticed on the walk-through with Rick and Thomas were all made for securing and disabling humans. There'd been nothing indicating parafolk were welcome or expected in Chris' little home away from home.

She was positioned so she straddled one of the padded benches. She'd bet it had been raised so her paws hovered above the floor, just far enough to prevent her from touching anything. Her muzzle pointed into the room, where she could see Thomas and Cristina. The other woman had pulled down the straps around her chest and was rubbing her bared breasts across his thighs.

Again the red glow of Thomas' eyes gave Harriet pause. What an idiot that woman was, to display herself so close to a vampire clearly in the throes of strong bloodlust. From the fierce expression Thomas wore, it was likely closer to a blood craze, although she'd never heard of such a thing.

Of course, until she met Rick and Thomas, she'd never known of psychic communication between the different types of parafolk. Her time spent with them had given her quite an education. Who knew what other unusual circumstances might exist?

While she watched, Cristina reached up and drew a fingernail from her shoulder down across her breast, almost to one nipple. A trail of red welled in its wake. The rich aroma of fresh blood cut through the mingled scents of disinfectant and old blood. Sweet Sol, if it was this strong to her nose, what would it do to Thomas?

The vampire roared and strained against his bonds. Harriet wondered if the silver alloy would hold, but Cristina ignored the vamp's reaction.

"I won't fuck you, Christian, but I would like you to help me out here. Provided it doesn't gross you out. Would you lick this up—slowly now!—and let our friend here see what he's missing?"

Chris watched the vamp struggle to get free. He never took his eyes off Thomas while he reached out and, with pudgy fingers, squeezed the cut until blood welled up and ran across his fingertips.

"Ow! That hurts!" Cristina glared at him.

"Sorry." There was no remorse in his apology. "Just trying to make him crazier."

Without breaking eye contact, Chris lowered his head and lapped at the blood. "Mmmm…you taste divine, my dear. If I'm not mistaken, B positive?"

Thomas snarled, his expression turning completely feral, and Harriet blanched. Even before, when they'd been in the shuttle and he'd turned to Rick for satisfaction, she'd seen evidence the vampire had preserved his normal personality under the influence of his intense need.

Not this time. Now he strained against the chain across his chest, the silver burning and blackening the sensitive skin, and Thomas didn't even appear to feel it. Looking into his radiant eyes, there was nothing left of the Thomas she knew and loved. He growled, a low horrible sound from deep in his throat, and his eyes glowed an even brighter red. He bared his fangs, saliva dripping from them.

Harriet wasn't sure if the display was involuntary or intentional—designed to frighten their captors—but it certainly scared her.

She was afraid one of the men she loved might very well lose his mind.

Chapter Fourteen

೫

"I've got a yacht on the ground, tucked under the trees near the compound." Elvie's voice was rich with satisfaction. "They're here. Just where we thought they'd be. Engine temperature indicates just over five hours since arrival."

Rick frowned at the airlock readout. "Any sensors you can detect?"

"Not yet. No, just the usual surveillance equipment that was here before." She paused. "I've patched in the recording we used before. They'll see what they expect to see…assuming they're even looking."

Rick pocketed his electronic toolkit and grabbed the remote viewer Elvie favored. "Ready to rescue our partners?"

"Let's do it."

He rolled his shoulders as the hatch cycled closed behind him. "Are you with me?"

"Yes, Ricky, I'm here." The voice from the handheld was tinny but definitely Elvie's. And no one else ever used that nickname for him.

The gardens were still tangled and neglected, but the whole compound had a more sinister feel as he crossed the courtyard. Maybe it was because he knew more about the place, its owner and its intended use. He resisted the urge to look around for observers, instead extending his psychic awareness into the area. He could sense no one watching, or even as far as a klick away.

The lock was different. Someone had reset the codes and it took him longer to work his magic. He had to tuck Elvie's handheld into his belt to free both hands.

"Ricky, can you plug me into that port?"

The muffled interruption made him drop his tool. Dammit, he was going to have to start over. He pulled the remote out and glared at the camera. "Elvie, I'm trying to concentrate here. What port?"

"There's a data port I could see, down near the power outlet. At least I think it's a data port."

He frowned and looked around. The smooth walls, similar to those inside the airlock, gleamed unbroken. He squatted down and peered at the base of the walls. There was a port there, a tiny connection box.

"Wait a minute, I'll have to find the right wire." He rummaged in his kit and came up with two candidates. One fit perfectly. "Here you go."

"Great—I'm in," she chirped. "Thanks! I can see—"

"No need for a running commentary, Elvie. I'll do my work, you do yours." To his relief, she shut up and he went back to the task of mastering the lock.

As the release snicked open, she broke her silence. "Oh poor guy!"

Rick paused with one foot inside the airlock. "What? Did you find Thomas?"

"No, but I know what happened to Guvnor. He's been overpowered and sequestered in a tiny subroutine. I'm trying to let him out now. I'm going to see how a couple of those beta test mil-spec apps I picked up a few days ago do the job. This is a good reason to break out my new toys."

"Elvie, they'll know we're here." He fought to keep panic out of his voice.

"No they won't." She was too calm. Didn't she understand the danger they were in?

"You sound awfully sure of yourself."

"I am."

The lights flickered and went out. He cursed and froze. They came back on. "What was that?"

"Guvnor's fighting with Mallet and his cronies." Pride filled her voice as well as a large measure of satisfaction. "We're beating them too."

* * * * *

"You're going to change, and you're going to change soon," Chris told Harriet. "I'm running out of patience."

Let him wait. She wasn't going to shed her wolf form simply because it was what he wanted. Once he said he wouldn't touch her while she was furry, she knew it was the only way she could save herself.

That didn't go for Cristina though. The stupid bitch was still playing with fire, goading Thomas into more of a blood fever.

Harriet had had to sever their link—he wasn't thinking at all, just broadcasting extreme emotions. Frustration. Lust. Hunger. She watched the vampire strain against his bonds, his expression showing just how deep into mania he'd fallen.

"He took a dart for you. Let's see just how you feel about him. Would you change to save him?" Chris held eye contact with her yet unerringly picked out a long knife from his cupboard. The blade gleamed in the light, broken here and there by old gore.

He crossed to where Thomas writhed against his restraints. With a shove, he moved Cristina out of the way.

"Hey, I wasn't finished with him!" she said indignantly.

Chris ignored her, addressing Harriet instead. "Will you change to save him? I can cut him deeply and let him bleed out. I can cut him lightly and make him heal himself, repeatedly. We can do that until one of you gives in. Either he'll die or you'll change." He drew the knife between the chains across the vampire's chest, tracing a bloody line across the skin beneath. "It's your choice."

Even without the link, Harriet could feel the hatred and hunger rolling off Thomas in thick waves. His eyes burned bright red now as he glared his fury at their captors.

"Or I could stake him outright. Want to watch him die, little wolf-bitch?"

Harriet squirmed on the bench. If only she could get free…

Maybe she should change to human form. Chris would have to loosen her bonds to get everything he wanted from her and once he did, she'd tear him apart.

Don't give in.

The thought came clearly through as Thomas reestablished the link. He locked eyes with her, eyes that while red were suddenly clear and sane.

A deep wave of relief swept through her. *I thought I'd lost you.*

Through the link she felt a wave of rage sweep through him, the bloodlust temporarily distracting him. She felt him fight the rage, using his strength of personality to control it and not let it control him.

His mental voice was shaky afterwards. *I'm not sure how much longer I can do that. But no matter what, don't make yourself vulnerable to him.*

I won't let him kill you. She was adamant about that and sent her determination through to him.

You don't have to. Forget me. I'd rather be dead than insane. His thoughts were choppy, as if he held onto his self-control by a hair. *Take them yourself.*

I can't get free.

You can. I can see. They supplemented silver cuffs with ropes — ropes you can break, cuffs for humans or werewolf paws. If you half change, you can pull free. He sent a mental image of her, strapped down on a leather bench, held with a combination of rope and the silver-alloy cuffs.

He was right. If she could shift enough to slip, she could break the ropes and slide free. But she could only shift partway, or the shape of the cuffs, which were sized for the woman she'd become, would trap her.

Chris picked up a long wooden stake. "It's time to choose, bitch."

Harriet eyed him through her wolfish eyes. *Then I choose this,* she thought, although she knew they wouldn't hear her.

She willed the change to come over her and moved swiftly as it swept through her limbs. She arched her back with her superior strength and the rope parted with a rending sound. As paws changed into hands and feet, her wrists and ankles slid free of the cuffs. She knelt on the bench and let the change recede again, leaving her back in her wolf form.

It happened so fast that neither Chris nor the blonde had time to react. Both stood gaping at her as the now empty silver cuffs clanked onto the floor and Harriet slid off the bench to stand before them. Chris hoisted the wooden stake at her and it must have seemed a formidable weapon to him, but to Harriet it looked like a toothpick.

Now she was free. Free of the remaining silver-tainted tranq. Free to follow the two rabbits as they fled. She gave them a wolfish grin and growled deep in her throat.

There was nothing left for them to do but run. Chris, the wisest of the pair, took off first then Cristina kicked off her stiletto heels and pelted after him into the corridor. Harriet howled her glee at the thrill of the chase. Her rabbits ran faster and she took off after them.

But not as a wild animal would, with no plan other than to catch its prey. The impetuous wolf within her gave way to her cold anger. As she bounded down the hall, claws clicking on the hard floor, Harriet reviewed the structure's floor plan in her head. She thought she remembered how to get to the airlock they'd come in. When they reached it, she would seal the two criminals inside and come back and free Thomas. Then and only then, once she knew he was safe, she would call the authorities.

Cristina faltered and Harriet nipped at her elbow, resisting the urge to rend the woman's flesh. Breath rasping in her lungs, the blonde doubled her efforts and caught up with Chris-kid. They almost wedged themselves in a doorway, each trying to beat the other through.

Harriet yipped her delight.

Her quarry popped out on the other side and ran on.

"Harriet!" Elvie's voice came from the ceiling speaker, pitched too low for human ears to hear.

She barked in response.

"Great! Bring them to us — we're at the entrance we used before."

Chris tried to open a door and it stuck fast. He tore at the latch, looking over his shoulder. Harriet snickered at the fear in his eyes. It came out as a growl. He gave up and followed Cristina down the open hallway to the left.

"We're helping you herd them. Just keep them moving. Guvnor will seal off the other routes."

Harriet dropped back a few steps and began to play with her prey. When they hesitated, she'd jump forward and nip at their heels. When they ran steadily, she kept pace behind and let them run. Every once in a while, she'd howl just for the fun of it. That always made them speed up.

When they paused, fear evident in their eyes, she reminded herself of Thomas' body and the marks the silver chains burned into his flesh. She thought about the strain he'd been under, the scent of blood and sexual frustration, his worry over what would happen to her combining to rob him of his mind. They'd driven him to the brink of madness.

Then she'd make a point of nipping harder than before, until they sped away from her.

When she mapped their progress in her head, she realized that Guvnor was taking them on a roundabout route to the airlock. He was either tiring them out or avoiding areas that were out of his control. Or both.

Either way, she was slowly but surely returning to the path they'd taken on their first visit. Stars but she loved the *Sleepwalker*'s crew. All three of them, including that impossible metallic bitch, Elvie.

Now that was a sobering thought, loving an AI. When did Elvie creep under her skin and get into her heart?

Too bad they had no future. Once they brought down the Chris-kids and wrapped up this adventure, Harriet would have to move on. She should be used to it by now, but the prospect of being alone again still hurt.

She rounded a corner and backpedaled, trying to stop as the open door to the airlock loomed before her. On her haunches, claws scrabbling uselessly on the smooth floor, she slid through the door into the airlock. The Chris-kids reached the outside door and began punching buttons and typing codes into the touch pad.

The panel snicked shut behind her. The outside door remained closed.

A high-pitched hiss filled the space, accompanied by a slight mist. Some sort of spray. All of the things Thomas had said about germ warfare and defending the installation came back to her. A shiver of fear spread through her.

Harriet whimpered and tried to change. Nothing happened to her limbs. Her vision wavered and she slipped into darkness.

Chapter Fifteen

&

"Guvnor, you idiot—Harriet's in there! You blew the timing on the door."

A deep, rough male voice came from the speakers. "She wasn't supposed to be that close behind them." The male AI sounded apologetic and a bit panicked. Rick couldn't blame him—he himself had been on the receiving end of Elvie's displeasure before.

"She's still recovering from the tranq, and now you've killed her!" Elvie swore like a jump booster who'd lost a cargo. The handheld Rick carried fairly glowed with her anger, every indicator on full power.

"No, Elvie, I didn't mean to. Her constitution should be stronger than that of the humans in there with her. And the gas I released is only to inhibit consciousness, not cease all functions. She'll recover, I promise."

Rick hid a smile. Guvnor was right. According to Rick's extended senses, Harriet was out cold but nowhere near death.

"She'd better, you incompetent mass of electrons." Elvie sniffed.

Rick wondered what she could do to his programming. Guvnor inhabited her world and Elvie liked being in control, which meant she could manipulate that world very well. Those toys she collected weren't all designed to mask their presence when they needed it. He'd wager Guvnor would find his abilities impaired the next time he tried to do, well, whatever it was AIs liked to do to…well…relax.

He felt a change in Harriet's psi signature just before Guvnor spoke. "She is stirring, Elvie. The humans are still unconscious." Relief filled Guvnor's voice.

Rick stopped pacing and tilted his head at the speaker in the ceiling. "Well, well, well, Elvie, you can't say you don't have tender feelings for Harriet, not after that attack on him for only knocking her out."

"Humph, like I'm supposed to ignore her contributions to this escapade? She saved Tommy's life. I can't hate her for that."

"Do you know he's still safe?"

"As I reported to you barely five minutes ago, he is unconscious but his health is improving. Don't worry, Ricky, I'm monitoring his condition. Respiration and heartbeat are slowing. Both are good signs."

"But what about what they were doing to him? From what was in Harriet's mind, they were driving him mad."

There was a long pause and when Elvie spoke again there was an uncertainty completely foreign to her voice. "All I can report on is his physical condition, Rick. His mind isn't something I can reach."

And he couldn't reach his longtime partner either. A tendril of fear drew tight around Rick's heart.

Guvnor spoke as Elvie finished. "I am evacuating the gas now. Mister Richard, it will be safe for you to enter in one minute, twenty seconds."

"Call me Rick, Guvnor." Rick tapped his hand on the wall beside the door, marking the time until he could retrieve at least one of his partners and verify the status of the other.

"As you wish, Rick."

* * * * *

Harriet's vision returned slowly, the blobs of colors before her resolving into the huddled shapes of the Chris-kids on the slick floor of the airlock. She inhaled deeply and the figures in front of her wavered. When she moved a limb, a paw swam into view. The last she remembered, she'd been chasing rabbits.

No, she'd been chasing her former captors. She couldn't suppress a wolfish grin.

"Welcome back, Harriet!" Elvie crowed. "Yippee! We did it!"

The door slid open and Harriet felt Rick's presence behind her. He knelt and pulled her into his arms. He buried his face in her ruff. "Thank God you're safe! I thought, no, I feared I'd lost you."

He smelled vaguely of concern and excitement, and strongly of home. She leaned into him. *You almost did.*

"Elvie's told me she's monitoring Thomas and that he's healing, but where is he?"

He's in the dungeon. Hung up, but alive. She hesitated. *He helped save me...showed me how to get free.*

Rick repeated that aloud for Elvie's benefit and added, "Guvnor took care of the Chris-kids. He and Elvie are quite a team."

"You helped too, Ricky."

As if. Don't let her fool you. If it weren't for her, I'd be toast back on Deltan, along with the Sleepwalker.

Harriet struggled to her feet. Rick let her do it, for which she was grateful. After the day she'd had, a girl needed to know she could stand on her own four feet. She stumbled out into the corridor. Rick followed and the panel slid shut behind him.

"Well, are you going to stay furry, Harriet, or change so we can talk like normal people?" Elvie's voice was tart.

Harriet growled. Like she was ever normal, even for a werewolf. But then Elvie didn't know that, did she? And Harriet wasn't about to tell her.

She pulled away from Rick and let the change come over her.

"Beautiful," Rick said as he grabbed her again and held her close. This time he kissed her. *I wasn't sure I'd ever do this again. Thanks the stars you're all right.*

She opened her mouth and welcomed his tongue. Sucking gently, she agreed. *And you and Thomas. And even Elvie.*

Elvie can hold her own. But speaking of Thomas, we'd better go free him. Rick reluctantly lifted his head. "Elvie, how's Thomas doing now?"

"He's still out. The sun is scheduled to rise in a few moments. You'll have to hurry and leave through a different exit. As a precaution, Guvnor's going to keep the perps shut in here."

"Not a problem, as long as you can guide us to it."

"Don't worry," Elvie assured them. "We've got the place entirely under our control. Do you need help from here?"

"I think I can find it." Harriet started off, pulling Rick by the hand. "And thanks, Elvie. You were right on time. I couldn't have planned it better."

"You're very welcome, Harriet." Elvie sounded smug. "And I've reviewed the logs Mallet recorded right up until we overpowered him. Thanks for trying to keep Thomas safe."

Rick caught up with her and wrapped an arm around her shoulders. "I think Elvie really likes you. You should have heard her when Guvnor let the gas get you — she was ready to rip his face off."

"I was not, Ricky," Elvie objected. "He doesn't have a face. And I don't go telling tales about you."

"I don't mind if you do, as long as they're good tales. I think it was sweet of you."

"You do?" Her tone softened.

"Yeah, well, I like you too, Elvie." Harriet reached back and patted Rick's ass. "But I lust you, Rick." She caught herself before she used Elvie's pet name for him. No sense in riling the AI just when she was coming around.

Rick smiled down at her. "Let's get Thomas. I think we need a tender reunion."

Harriet slipped her hand into his back pocket and squeezed. "Or not so tender."

"Then let's hurry!" He laughed, more carefree than she'd heard him before. They began to run.

"Rick, Harriet, I've got an incoming ship. Heavily armed." Elvie's voice held an edge of panic. "We can't possibly stand up—oh wait, it's the cops. Sent by Bernie!" She chuckled. "The accounting army to the rescue!"

"Hey, don't diss accountants…that's my vocation!"

"There's nothing left but the cleaning up," Rick told her. "We'll let them take out the trash. In the meantime, we've got a reunion to plan." He directed Harriet toward the dungeon where their third still waited.

"It won't be any kind of a reunion, at least not the way you want. You're not going to have time," Elvie sniffed. "The military-type goons need to speak with you. All of you."

Harriet stopped in her tracks as they arrived to view Thomas still hanging in his chains. She chilled as Rick's jovial expression disappeared and his face grew grim.

Neither of them could sense anything in the mind of their vampire lover.

"No one is going to be speaking to him now. He's lost in the bloodlust." Rick shook his head and turned to Harriet. "Can you get him out of here on your own?"

She was strong enough to carry him. Harriet nodded slowly.

Rick handed the comm-unit to her. "Elvie, direct her the way to the back entrance."

"Will do, Rick." Even the AI sounded somber, for once using his proper name.

Harriet leaned over Thomas and draped one limp arm over his shoulder. With one swift motion, she picked up the vampire and cradled him against her chest. "Come on, let's go. I'd really like to see the last of this place."

"Me too." Rick said. "But I'll have to stay and talk to the authorities."

Harriet glanced around to make sure they hadn't forgotten anything. The only splash of color in the sterile hallway was a brilliant scarlet buckle on the floor. The memory of Cristina in the cat suit made her shudder.

If not for Thomas' immense control and presence of mind, neither of them would have survived being tortured by those sick puppies. No, they were rabbits, she reminded herself and indulged in a short grin. That was a good chase, even if it had ended differently than she liked. For what they'd done to Thomas, she'd gladly have torn them limb from limb.

Forget them, Harriet love. We've got better things to do. Like tucking our partner safely into his bunk.

Harriet nodded. *How will we bring him out of it?*

It can be done…with love and patience. Mostly love.

Love as in sex? You're thinking what I'm thinking. The soft purple glow of his desire opened up in front of her. She wrapped the green of her mind around him and the purple flared brighter.

Definitely. Rick smiled slightly. "It will take both to get him back to us."

Chapter Sixteen

ഇ

When Harriet set his sleeping form on the bunk, Thomas curled around a pillow without waking. Harriet drew a blanket up over him.

"He can't feel that," Elvie said.

"I know, but it makes me feel better. And he'll appreciate it when he wakes up."

"When he wakes up, he isn't going to know you. He'll be in full lust for blood and sex." Elvie's voice broke. "He'll be completely out of his mind, Harriet."

Harriet straightened, setting her jaw. "Then we'll have to bring him back into his mind," she said, putting all the determination she felt into the words. She reached out to his mind, feeling the hard wall that protected it. He'd drawn deep within himself, shutting out the outside world. The entire outside world, including her and Rick. She stroked the hair out of his face, hoping her gentle touch would ease the horror raging through him.

"Has he ever been this way before?" She hated asking the question and admitting to the AI that she didn't know just what to do, but she needed to learn what she was up against. What she'd seen of Thomas in bloodlust before, when he'd nearly attacked Rick in the shuttle, hadn't prepared her for this.

"I've never seen him this deep before," Elvie admitted. "In the past, he always knew when to let go of the fury so that it wouldn't build up. This time he had no way to let it go."

"He was lucid for a few moments. He showed me how to escape. I could feel the strain he was under though."

The AI was quiet for a long time. "Perhaps you should go eat. I've pulled a nice juicy steak for you."

The steak she'd been promised earlier, after Elvie had pulled that trick on her back on Deltan, not warning her that multiple moons would be full. Harriet almost laughed. It seemed a long time ago and yet it was only a day or two.

"I can't remember the last time I ate either," she said softly. "I never did catch that rabbit."

"The Chris-kid rabbits? You wouldn't have wanted to eat them anyway. Indigestion for sure."

Harriet did laugh but curled up next to Thomas. "I'm not really that hungry yet. I'll stay with him until Rick gets back."

Elvie sounded sympathetic. "Very well. I'll put the steak on hold for later. As soon as Rick comes aboard, we'll take off and get out of the sun's influence. Then—we'll see what happens."

Yes they would. Harriet sent the thought directly against the solid wall that covered Thomas' mind. *I'm going to help you, lover, if I have to fuck the madness out of you.*

With the strain of the day, she fell asleep next to Thomas, wrapping herself around his still body, hoping that when he woke she and Rick together would be able to restore him.

It was an hour later when Rick slipped into the bed and woke her. He kept his expression neutral but she felt his worry right through that, concern about the still-comatose vampire

"Elvie is lifting off now. We'll have about twenty minutes until he wakes." He handed her the silver-plated handcuffs. "Let's get him ready." In terse words he explained just what they were going to have to do to bring sanity back to their friend.

Nodding, Harriet secured Thomas to the bed. As she did she heard Rick lean over and whisper into the vampire's ear, not even trying a mental connection. She almost smiled as she heard him make nearly the same promise she'd made.

"Thomas, you hear me? We'll bring you back if we have to fuck you senseless to do it."

* * * * *

Fire...his skin was on fire, his blood flaming in his veins. Heat scorched his face, his mouth and particularly his loins...his cock was on fire. Inside his mind, Thomas was engulfed by the flames, the heat, the blaze of lust, bloodlust, the need for sex and blood burning through him.

He was lost to it. Thomas slid further back into the walled sanctuary of his mind, the flames, heat and lust burning outside, but here he was safe. Here the sensations from the outside dimmed to a bearable level. Here he could keep himself together.

Part of him wanted to break free of the fire and the flames, part wasn't sure he could. Part of him was certain that only agonizing pain dwelt outside the barriers of his mind.

Thomas?

Another's voice in his mind, reaching out to him. A female voice, strong with green overtones, red flames of passion underneath.

A female. His female, he remembered, his and his partner's. His female friend, his lady lover. She was here, the lady werewolf who'd been chained near him, who'd gotten free and driven the bad ones away.

Harriet...that was her name. She'd been willing to sacrifice herself to rescue him and he'd talked her out of it.

She was here with him. Thomas tried to reach out to her through the flames but was beaten back by the pain. It hurt out there and he was so tired of hurting. So easy to stay where he was.

And when had he taken the easy way? Answer—never.

Of course it was possible it wasn't his female here with him. There had been another woman torturing him, cutting his skin, cutting her own. She'd been very aroused by it, the stench of her drenched pussy warring with the scent of blood. Perhaps that was the woman he sensed with him.

He opened his mind a little, waiting for the assault on his senses, waiting for the scent of blood, both old and fresh, mixed with the cloying musky odor of arousal, the smell he remembered coming from the evil female with the knife that had seared his flesh.

Instead he smelled something sweeter, fresh. The scent of a woman he was familiar with. He breathed in deeply, his cock tensing over the smell.

There was more as well, more than scent. A soft crooning slid into his ears, the sound of a woman being loved. With that sound came another, a man breathing hard and fast. A couple in the bed next to him.

A couple fucking.

Thomas growled a warning, feeling his eyes flash to red. He still couldn't see. Everything was blurry as the bloodlust still coursed through him, but he didn't need sight to know what was happening. Someone else had his cock inside the female he wished to claim as his own and he didn't like that.

He tried to rise, but strong bonds held him fast to the bed. The couple next to him shifted slightly. He could now smell the rich scent of the man, also familiar, but it was the woman who drew him. He growled again. He needed sex and blood, hot and fresh.

Warm lips slid along his neck, pointed teeth nipping at him.

Again he growled. A hand closed over his cock and gave it a stroke that threw him against his bonds again. Frustration hissed out of him, fury that he wasn't able to break free.

Warm lips slid down his torso, teeth nibbling lightly, and a tongue played briefly with his nipples. Thomas snarled. This was foreplay. He didn't need foreplay, he needed sex, raw naked sex, right now.

The lips and tongue reached his cock and fastened onto them. Thomas sighed inside his mind. That was more like it. He arched his back, driving his cock into his lover's mouth. Female, he thought. No hint of beard stubble such as he was used to with Rick.

Rick…that's who was with Harriet, his lover Rick. That was the familiar smell, Rick in rut. The smell of semen and precum – Rick's smell.

Thomas tried to relax into his bonds, his attempt thwarted by the pull of someone's mouth drawing him deeper and deeper. He couldn't relax when someone made love to him that way.

Arching his back again, he drove his cock into the waiting mouth, hot and moist. For long moments that was all he needed, being sucked on.

Until it wasn't enough. He needed more.

A shuffling took place next to him, and the mouth on him disappeared. Someone straddled his hips, placing themselves over him, holding his cock upright until an incredibly sweet, warm and tight place slid over him, encasing him in heat. Thomas moaned his pleasure over that, knowing it was his woman's cunt enclosing him. She lifted and he slid out, but then she pushed down over him, repeating the action, setting up a rhythm that kept time with his heartbeat. She sped up and his heart did as well.

Fucking, fucking good. He moaned aloud and reached for her, but his hands didn't move, bound by the handcuffs on his wrists.

Gods, he needed to touch her, to caress her. He needed to feel her skin.

He needed to taste her blood. Companion blood later, but now he needed her more. NOW.

Something moved across his field of vision. He felt his wrists lifted and the cuffs fell away. Thomas reached to grab

Harriet by the shoulders, pulling her down to him. His mouth searched for hers, finding her, binding them together in a kiss.

A moment later his ankles were similarly freed. Now he could move as he wished. Thomas turned, taking her with him and under him. He drove into her with hard jerks, harder than he usually allowed, afraid he might injure his lover.

In his mind came Harriet's mental voice. *You can't hurt me this way, lover.*

And he knew he couldn't. She was a werewolf, stronger than any human, strong enough even for him at his roughest. He thrust far harder than he'd ever allowed himself before, something that might have broken the pelvis of a normal woman.

Harriet wasn't normal and thank the stars for that. She moaned and wrapped her legs around his thighs, pulling them apart.

Then he felt her hands on the globes of his buttocks, pulling them apart as well. A familiar hand fondled the tight bud of his ass, teasing it with something cool and slick. Fingers. Lubed fingers. A welcome and familiar touch.

Something hot and slick took the place of the fingers and that too was very familiar. He gritted his teeth as a hard long cock slid implacably into his anal canal, past the first ring of muscle and the second, pausing to press hard against his prostrate.

Gule's fleck! Him inside of Harriet, Rick inside of him. Penetrated and penetrating at the same time. It was the ultimate fantasy. It was his ultimate joy.

The three of them moved as one, and all sighed and moaned their pleasure. They were a threesome, three making love as one. A beast with three backs, and triple the pleasure between them.

He bit down on Harriet's neck, sucking at her blood. Not a companion's, but it served to ease the need, reinforcing his precious and fragile control. Rick's wrist slid into his view. *Take what is needed, my love.*

His love. His, and Harriet's, and he was theirs. Thomas bit into Rick's wrist, tasting the rich blood flowing down his throat, helping mend all that was wrong with him. He stroked long and hard into Harriet, felt Rick stroke hard into him.

Felt their minds link with his, in a green, gold and purple concatenation.

All three came simultaneously, the orgasms multiplying each other until none could have picked just who came first or last or even best. It was enough that they all came. Together. As they were meant to be.

Later on, Harriet returned to a thinking state of mind when she lay next to Thomas, cradling him on her chest as Rick nuzzled his back.

"I love you both so much," Thomas said, for once completely serious. "Let me give you companion marks, Harriet. Rick, I know you were here first, but would you mind?"

Rick lifted his head. "Stars, no, not if it keeps our lovely furry female with us on a permanent basis. You know, Harriet, I like having you around."

"Elvie, you're also a partner here. Do you have any objections to Harriet joining your crew permanently?" Thomas asked.

"About time you asked my opinion," the AI grumbled. "I think she'd be nuts to leave. She belongs here. With us."

"See? Even Elvie can see how perfect you are for us. We all want you to stay."

It took an effort for Harriet to keep her mind on what Thomas wanted, especially when he lowered his head and took a nipple in his mouth. The scrape of a fang across tender skin was too distracting. All she wanted at the moment was to suck and fuck, and be sucked and fucked by, these two men.

"I'm not sure I'm ready for that," she hedged. It took a lot of effort not to stiffen and pull away.

"You're not?" Disappointment radiated from the vampire's open mind, echoed by Rick's. She raised her mental shields and closed herself off from them. She reminded herself that these were her best friends, her lovers and her partners.

And they didn't know what she was.

They didn't know the truth. If they did, no way would they cuddle up to her this way, showing her glimpses of what the rest of the universe enjoyed with their mates. They didn't deserve to be the destiny of a creature like her—hell, even she didn't know exactly what she was. Without knowing her origins, how could she agree to join them?

Rick moved, sliding his cock over her clit like a violin bow. The note of ecstasy he played went on and on as he took forever to glide out. She whimpered when he paused, the thick head of his shaft lodged just inside. After a moment of trembling, he began the long, slow thrust back inside her.

She couldn't keep her hands from clutching uncontrollably at the bedclothes. "Oh gods, don't ever stop."

Thomas lifted his head. A smear of blood marred his chin. When had he bitten her? She hadn't felt it. "As you wish, sweetheart." He pinched her nipple and a tiny drop of blood welled up. "You are so tasty."

She drew his head back to her breast. "And you've got to be hungry."

"All in good time. Anticipation is half the fun."

Rick stopped in mid-thrust to stare at him. "Whoa! Who are you and what have you done with the selfish, impatient vampire I know and love?"

"You love my impatience? Really?" Thomas leaned forward until he was nuzzling Rick's neck. "In that case, forget the anticipation." *Just a little, to hold me until you're both ready.* He grabbed Rick's balls in one hand and Harriet's breast in the other and bit down.

The rich flavor of blood washed across Harriet's tongue, even without a direct link. She sighed and swallowed as if she were the one drinking from Rick's throat.

Rick moaned and thrust, filling her pussy. She arched into the grip Thomas had on her nipple and groped for his cock. No sense in having her hands free when there were so many male body parts unattended.

The future could take care of itself for a while.

"Wakey, wakey!" The chirpy greeting brought all three of them awake.

"What is it, Elvie?"

"You've got company." There was an excited lilt in her voice.

She sounded too happy for it to be a stranger. Thomas raised a brow at Rick. *Any ideas?*

Rick frowned. *Nope. I'm not picking up anything at all.*

"Who is it, Elvie?"

"A surprise." At the AI's smug tone, the two men exchanged glances with Harriet, who was still blinking in the low cabin lights. "The ship is about four klicks out and closing slowly. I estimate you have time for a quick shower but no fooling around."

Rick shook his head. *Still out of range. We'll have to let Elvie have her fun, at least until whoever it is comes aboard.*

Aloud Thomas said, "Elvie, are we still on course for Toolat? When do we have to be there?"

"Yes. You're due to report in six standard hours."

From her clipped answer, he knew she was multitasking. "Still in communication with Guvnor?"

"Yes. I've got no time for chitchat, Tommy, and neither have you. Get moving!"

"Aye-aye, ma'am." He jumped from the bed. "I get the shower first!"

Over the drone of the sonic cleanser, he listened to Harriet and Rick talk. He loved the two of them more than he thought was possible. So much it unsettled him.

What would he do if one of them died? It could have happened the day before. Rick could have been killed in the detonation of the ship that the Chris-kids set up. Harriet could have died at Christian's hands — but then he most likely would have died with her.

All the more reason to bind her to him. He and Rick both needed her. Why was she so damned reluctant to accept them? It was more than she was saying, he was certain. She'd closed herself off to them since he'd mentioned making her his companion. He needed to get to the bottom of this, for the sake of his sanity.

He watched her face as he strode back into the cabin, nude and erect. The way she ogled his cock was reassuring.

So it wasn't that she didn't love him. He already knew that, from having merged with her mind. He knew almost everything about her, and it was frustrating not even to be able to see the barrier that kept her from making a complete commitment.

Gule's fleck, what was the werewolf's problem?

Was it the fact that she was a shifter? Or that weird psi power she had? He'd never heard of any shifters having the abilities of other parafolk. Whatever it was, he was determined to overcome her objections. However long it took, he and Rick would do it.

They had no choice. She was their missing piece.

Guests on the *Sleepwalker* were rare. He wanted to look his best, both for company and for Harriet and Rick. By the time he'd chosen a fresh jumpsuit and zipped himself into it, Harriet and Rick were both out of the shower and dressed. Together they climbed down to the bridge.

"About time," Elvie greeted them. A monitor sprang to life and filled with a close-up shot of a hull. "There's the ship."

"That view's a bit close, isn't it?" Rick reached for the panel.

"She's already docked with us. We were just waiting for you to saunter out of your cabin."

"Then why didn't you send us to the main hatch?" Thomas frowned and set off back down the corridor, pulling Harriet along behind. "I don't like strangers wandering around my ship!"

"I am the ship, Tommy." The AI's tone was tart. "Besides, this isn't a stranger."

They rounded the corner and stopped. A petite, middle-aged human brunette in a dark blue business suit—she could have been one any of the corporate drones they'd met in the past—stood patiently by the airlock. Whatever Elvie's claims to the contrary were, Thomas had never seen her before.

Harriet shrieked, swept past him and gathered the woman into a hug.

"Although we've never met formally, I don't feel that we're strangers." Bernie LaJunta's sexy voice filled the space around them. Her liquid brown eyes met his over Harriet's shoulder. Her voice and smile zinged along his nerve endings, making every bit of his libido stand up and take notice. He tried not to gape. "You must be Thomas."

"Of course, and this is Rick." Thomas pulled the tatters of his concentration around himself and sketched a bow. "We owe you a great debt."

"It has been paid in full. I have a lot to tell you."

Rick shook himself and spoke. "Then shall we sit down and make ourselves more comfortable?" He glanced at Thomas. "I think the lounge is the best place. Elvie, can you—"

"Already ordered. Bernie likes the same tea you do, Ricky, and the cookies are just about done."

"Thank you so much, Elvie! And have you made contact with Argent?"

"Yes, Bernie, and she's as delightful as you said."

So that's why Elvie had been distracted. She was no doubt getting to know and catching up with her "sister" in Bernie's household. Thomas bowed again and let Rick and Bernie precede him. Harriet was still wrapped around Bernie like a ribbon.

He busied himself getting them all settled in the lounge. He and Rick had to settle for sitting next to each other. Harriet was glued to Bernie's side.

"Very nice," Bernie praised the refreshments.

"Thank you," Elvie simpered. "I've just given Argent the instructions. A little token of my appreciation."

"I'm honored again by your kindness, Elvie."

Thomas hadn't believed Rick when he said that Bernie had conquered the prickly AI in only a few minutes. Now he understood.

"Well, let's get down to business." Bernie folded her hands in front of her and leaned forward. "Right now, I am in the company of heroes. Expect to see your names and pictures in news vids everywhere over the next few days.

"You four have managed to break open a case that has baffled the auditors for months. We've traced transactions through the system and lost them every time. Someone was fiddling with the records but we couldn't pinpoint just who it was."

"So Harriet's old boss was involved in more than just the vaccine smuggling and planetary takeover business?" Rick bit into a cookie.

"Yes. Add embezzlement, smuggling, insider trading, outright theft, kidnapping, torture, rape and murder and a few other felonies here and there. You provided us with detailed evidence that he was moving up a few levels in his criminal career, planning genocide on Deltan.

"As far as your ship's mortgage goes, that was an offshoot of his loan skimming operation, we think a recent development. He saw an opportunity to ensure the colonists didn't survive and get his hands on the vaccine shipment at the same time. If the plague got out of control, he had a bolt hole all ready."

"And how did he cover his tracks so thoroughly?" Harriet asked.

"He'd been working with an accomplice in IT who disappeared when the case became public. He was picked up at home, stuffing credits into a suitcase and irradiating data crystals. There were enough left for us to piece together his role in things. We hadn't looked at that particular department, since he wasn't in a job that would normally have access to the records we were examining. But he'd held several different positions over the years and he hoarded passwords and access codes."

She sipped her tea. "The best thing was that I now have a new job. Two actually. I now run the entire audit practice at Galaxy. And I've been offered a seat on the board of Mullens & Forth, the largest auditing partnership in Sector Five."

"Wow! That's a plum!" Harriet breathed. Her eyes were wide and riveted on Bernie.

"Harriet, honey, I know you've wanted a desk job for quite a while and right now you're at loose ends. It'll take some time—thank goodness it's not my responsibility!—to unravel and then rebuild your old department. I'd like this opportunity to steal you away and have you work for me. As the new head of Auditing at Galaxy, I'd like you to take my old job. I am officially offering you a position as Lead Auditor for Collateralized Long-Term Loans."

"That's fabulous!" Harriet grinned through her sniffles. "I can't believe it. You've just handed me the job I always knew I was born to do."

Thomas could feel her slipping out of their lives. He looked at Rick in dismay. *How are we supposed to compete with Harriet's dream job?*

We can't. We'll have to find a way to hang around.

But we belong out there, between the stars. And so does she. Even as he expressed the thought, he had to grimace at his selfishness. Stars, he could be such an asshole.

That's just one of the things I love about you, Rick mentally snickered. *We'll find a way to stay with her. We have to – we three were meant to be together.*

Bernie took Harriet's hands in hers and smiled. "Oh, honey, believe it. And you'll have your work cut out for you. Right now, the most important project on your new desk is the reconstruction of all those mortgages that Balhooey was skimming. It's going to require a lot of forensic accounting."

Harriet's eyes lit up. Thomas could almost see the enthusiasm bubbling up inside her. She fairly glowed. Gee, she really had liked unraveling their accounts and payments that first night.

"All the data will come to you, so there's no traveling, but I imagine you've had enough of that in the past week."

"Well," Harriet looked at Rick and Thomas. "I don't know about that. The traveling wasn't so bad. The company was the best. And we did a lot of good."

Rick spoke before Thomas could stop him. "Harriet, it's your dream! You have to do it. We'll find some kind of work. You haven't seen the last of us, don't worry."

Idiot! Why do you have to encourage her?

How can I not? I love her.

The stark simplicity of Rick's reply took Thomas aback. What kind of a lover had he become? Selfish and impatient, as he'd always been. He mentally shrugged off the self-criticism. As long as he kept Harriet, he didn't care what anyone called him.

And I love both of you, Harriet assured them. *How can I refuse this? But I don't want to tie you both down too.*

Before Thomas could answer her through their link, Bernie spoke. "And the best news is, for you, Thomas and Rick, that in appreciation of your assistance and great courage, Galaxy is forgiving your debt. Completely. As of today, you own the *Sleepwalker* outright."

Elvie cheered.

Thomas and Rick high-fived Harriet.

Bernie beamed.

"I don't want to leave you."

Bernie cleared her throat. "I suggest you speak to Clara Thompson who heads Galaxy's HR department. There might be something open that would suit you."

Thomas couldn't deny the hope in Harriet's eyes. "Thanks, Bernie. We'll call her tomorrow."

What are we gonna do, sweep the floors?

If we have to. I'm not letting her go.

Chapter Seventeen

ಐ

Thomas followed Rick into the galley and watched his companion pour a large glass of Charon brandy and drink it down in one gulp. He winced as his friend refilled the glass and hoped this one would be sipped instead of guzzled.

Rick a little fuzzy was a lot of fun. Rick on a bender wasn't. Fortunately the psi sat down heavily on a stool and contemplated the contents of his glass without drinking. He looked up Thomas. "Want some?"

Thomas shook his head. "I'll get some from you later…if you're conscious enough for it."

Rick glared but shoved his glass aside. "I just didn't think having a straight job would be so…so…"

"Boring," Thomas finished for him, taking the seat opposite.

"Boring is definitely the word. And frustrating. And…"

"And not what we really want to do." Thomas sighed and ran his hand through his shoulder-length dark hair. His new "boss" had even told him he should get it trimmed up to meet corporate standards. It wouldn't do for him to look like a miscreant while off chasing bad guys.

Fracking bounty hunters! came Rick's thoughts. *That's what the company wants us for.*

It isn't so bad, Thomas replied in kind. *After all, that's what Harriet used to do.*

And she hated it. All she wanted was a desk job where she could work with numbers.

And now she has that. We agreed to this so we could be with her.

"But even that's going to be only once in a while!" Rick said aloud. "She's going to be working here while we get sent all over the place."

Thomas sighed. "These were the only jobs available…it isn't like we're trained for high finance. We spend a few months doing this and work on convincing Harriet she needs to be with us. Maybe leaving her behind will work in our favor. Make her miss us."

"More likely make her realize she's better off without us. Think about it, we nearly got her raped and killed."

"Her boss had it in for her way before we came along. If anything, we helped save her sweet little furry rump."

Rick laughed shortly. "Trust you to look on the bright side. I just wish she'd commit to us…or at least tell us why she doesn't want to."

"She will eventually." Thomas grabbed his partner's arm. "Come with me."

"Where?"

"To my cabin. You need a good fuck."

"Aren't we going to wait for Harriet?"

"In your mood? I think you need to take the edge off or you'll end up barking at her and that's the last thing we need."

The first glass of brandy must have finally hit. Rick gave Thomas a goofy smile. "Me bark? Isn't that our furry lady's area of expertise?"

"We've made her howl and we've made her whimper, my friend. But never bark. Come on, Rick, there's a blowjob waiting for you."

Minutes later Thomas had Rick on his back with his eyes closed in bliss and was enthusiastically sucking his cock when Harriet opened the door. She paused in the doorway, "Elvie said you were here…" but her voice trailed off as she noticed what they were up to. "I'm sorry…didn't mean to interrupt…"

she said weakly, leaving the door open as she backed out of the room.

Immediately Thomas was off the bed, Rick's cock falling forgotten as he raced after her. A werewolf was fast, but a vampire was faster. Even as she ran full speed down the corridor, Thomas threw his arms around her and swept her up. It was a testament to how upset she was that he was able to keep his hold on her and carry her back to his room.

He dumped her onto the bed next to Rick who was now sitting up, caressing his own cock. "What's the idea of running away, sweetheart?"

"You were doing all right on your own."

"Of course we were," Thomas interjected. "But that doesn't mean you weren't welcome to join us." He threw his arms around her and buried his nose in her neck. "You smell so good."

Harriet stiffened but quickly softened in his embrace and rubbed his back. "You smell like brandy."

He chuckled. "Want some?"

"Maybe."

Something was bothering her, Thomas could tell, but Harriet's mind was as closed off as Rick's used to get. Sometimes a little bit of drink helped free up the truth. "I have an idea. You two wait here."

He left them cuddling and when he got back with the brandy for them and a bottle of serum-nol for himself, they'd progressed to undressing each other. He stopped for a moment and let the sight of the two of them warm him. His two special people, both strong and beautiful, kissing and caressing each other. Giving each other pleasure. That's what a triad was all about, having two people to love.

Pouring three glasses, he interrupted Harriet and Rick and passed brandy to them while keeping the serum-nol for himself. "I'd like to propose a toast."

"A toast?" Harriet looked wary.

"To us. To the future."

Thomas sipped his drink while Rick drank happily. Harriet looked at the two of them, shrugged and sipped hers. "Hmm…" she said appreciatively. "Real Charon brandy." She took a deeper drink and some of her apprehension seemed to melt away.

"Only the best is worth drinking." Rick lifted his glass. "To the future and the lady we want to spend it with."

Thomas nodded. "To our lady." He and Rick drank.

Harriet didn't. She played with her glass and examined the contents as if it held some hidden truth. "I heard about your jobs."

Rick's smile faltered a little. "Another thing to drink to."

"Or drink for." She looked at him. "You can't really like the idea of being bounty hunters."

"It's not that bad."

"I guess. You'll at least have each other when you're gone."

Thomas suddenly realized why she'd been so upset at finding them having sex. "You thought we'd be happy with just the two of us to share a bed? No, Harriet, we need more than that. We need you."

"Yeah, we need you," Rick finished his brandy and put the glass on the floor. He tugged Harriet into his arms. "Without you…well, it just isn't the same."

"That's why we're taking the jobs, so we can be with you."

"So we can talk you into staying with us. Be our mate."

"Mate?" Harriet looked at both of them. "You mean a real mate? Like…" her voice broke off. "Like having kids?"

"Kids?" Thomas shook his head. "I'm afraid I can't give you kids…"

"But I can!" Rick finished for him. His grin looked almost as wolfish as Harriet's did sometimes. "If that's what you wanted, I'd give you a litter of kids...or cubs or whatever."

Harriet looked stricken. "But I can't be with you. Not like that. You don't understand..." Suddenly she was out of his arms, on her feet and ready to run from the room again. In unison Thomas and Rick grabbed the tools their new jobs had gifted them with. In a heartbeat she was back on the bed, silver handcuffs on her ankles and wrists, both men holding her down.

The handcuffs had turned out to be the one bright point of their new job...now they had their own instead of having to borrow Harriet's. That also meant between them they had two pairs of restraints. She struggled against them but couldn't get free with both of them on top of her. Finally she gave up.

"Let me go."

"Not until you answer a few questions, Harriet," Rick said. He didn't sound as intoxicated as he had a few minutes before.

In response she began to struggle again. They both leaned into her.

Rick pushed his face close to hers. "Just why is it you don't think you can be with us? We love you, you love us. If you don't want a child, that's fine. If you do, that's fine too—whatever you want will be fine so long as you want us. And I don't have to be a psychic to know you do want us, so what's the fracking problem?"

Not quite the way Thomas would have put it, but it got the point across.

She stopped struggling long enough to glare at him. "What makes you think I want you?"

"Give it a rest!" Rick rolled his eyes. "Would we even be having this conversation if I didn't know that you love me and Thomas as much as anyone can love anyone else? I know you love me and him as much as I love you."

"And I love you too, Harriet darling," Thomas interjected. "So why don't you just tell us what the problem is?"

Her head fell back against the mattress and her eyes closed. "I can't have kids with you...or anyone."

Thomas shook his head. "That doesn't matter."

"It matters to me," she said. She turned her head away and he had to strain his heightened hearing to understand her next words. "I'm a rogue."

As serious as this subject was, Thomas had to laugh. "So are we."

She turned back and stared at him. "Not like I am. My grandmother was, well, she was part of an experiment. Genetic manipulation. That's what gives me psi powers. The same powers you have, Rick, only for you they're normal. Mine are a result of what some mad scientist did a hundred years back. Playing god to see if he could build a plague-resistant werewolf. I can't be sure I won't pass on what I am to my offspring."

"Whoa!" Rick held up his hand. "Wait a minute. What I said about kids holds. If we didn't have kids, I wouldn't have a problem with it, but if we did, so what if they were part werewolf and part psi? I certainly wouldn't care."

"And neither would I," Thomas spoke softly. "I'd love to have a couple of half-furry cubs running around here. We want you, Harriet, just as you are. In fact, that mad scientist may have been playing god for all the wrong reasons, but he managed to create the perfect woman for us. You...are...perfect! In every way."

Harriet pulled away to stare at him and then at Rick as if she couldn't believe what she was hearing. "But I'm not normal..."

Thomas burst into laughter again. "What *is* normal, Harriet? I'm a male vampire who lives with a male psi, and both of us want you, a werewolf woman. Stars, let's throw Elvie in for good measure...we live on a ship controlled by the bossiest AI in existence. Normal doesn't even come close to describing what we are...we're all rogues but somehow we make a perfect family."

"A perfect family." Harriet said the words softly, and Thomas thought he saw tears in her eyes. "All my life I've wanted to belong to a family."

"And you do, Harriet our love," Rick said quietly. "You belong with us."

She did start to cry. Rick gathered her into his arms while Thomas removed the restraints. Then they both held her, loving her with hands, arms and mouths, stroking her and kissing away her tears. Quickly the caresses went from comforting to sensual until they had removed her clothing and all three of them were ready to get back to having sex.

"Now where were we?" Rick said. "Oh yeah, Thomas was sucking my cock." He pushed Thomas down to that neglected member, which didn't look the least bit sad at having been forgotten. It perked up nicely as soon as Thomas got close enough to breathe on it.

"As for you, Harriet, come here." He pulled her into his arms. "I really want to suck on those luscious tits of yours."

She smiled as his head dipped between her breasts, then let out a low moan as one plump nipple disappeared between his lips. Thomas teased Rick's cock while his friend worshiped their woman's breasts.

This play went on for a while until Thomas decided he needed someone to suck his cock. Pulling off Rick, he drew Harriet into his arms, lifting her so she was balanced on his shoulders. Rick blinked at him as he took his first sip of Harriet's pussy.

There's a cock just within reach, Rick.

Oh. Okay.

Thomas felt Rick's lips close over the head of his cock and murmured appreciatively into Harriet's clit. She seemed to like that. Her hands grasping his shoulders for balance, she threw her head back and gave one of those inhuman cries of hers.

A werewolf in love, howling her passion. Thomas' cock pulsed at the sound and he knew Rick's did as well. They were pleasing *their* woman.

Harriet couldn't believe what was happening. She'd told them the one thing she'd been afraid they would find out and they'd accepted it as if it weren't a big deal. In fact they welcomed her...their "perfect" woman.

She was loved and accepted—and being made love to. Thomas' mouth worked with exquisite care to tease her clit and pussy into a state of extreme need. Every time he did that little sucking bit using the tip of his fang that way, all she wanted to do was howl.

And they didn't even mind that. In their minds all she sensed was deep satisfaction at making her howl. More carefree than she'd ever felt before, she gave in to that urge, letting go of her inhibitions.

All of her inhibitions, so that when she felt Rick's exploratory finger gently fingering her anus, she didn't say no. Didn't resist at all. His finger grew bolder, teasing her virgin opening so skillfully that she almost forgot what Thomas was doing with his mouth.

Almost. Thomas must have realized he had competition for her attention and stepped up his efforts. Of course he knew when her attention wandered from him. They were completely connected.

What a delightful situation to be in...caught between two lovers competing to make her feel so very, very good.

Rick pulled her off Thomas' shoulders and onto the bed in front of him. Pushing her up on all fours, he took over where Thomas had left off, licking her from behind, his fingers paying attention to her clit but his tongue never straying all that far from her anus. Thomas' cock bobbed up before her and

Harriet decided it looked like it needed attention so she took hold of it. Thomas moaned as she took him into her mouth, putting all her skill into pleasing him with the same intensity he'd used on her.

She reached out to his mind, golden haze streaked with passion. She also sought the purple of Rick's mind and they merged with hers, green, purple and gold, in a kaleidoscope display. She felt how Thomas liked having his cock sucked and felt the urgency in Rick's mind. She also felt how anxious he was.

She knew what he wanted but wasn't going to give in just yet. Let the man sweat a little, it would be good for him. She hid what she was thinking from him.

In the meantime, Thomas was feeling more and more like a man on the edge of climax. She leaned into him, pushing him onto his back. He went willingly and now his cock stood straight up, waving proudly. Harriet moved away from Rick and crouched over Thomas, lowering herself onto his staff. He moaned his appreciation. Rising up and down, Harriet soon brought Thomas close to climax, but she held off.

Uh, Harriet…I don't suppose… Rick's mental voice sounded both tentative and plaintive.

I imagine you know where Thomas keeps his lube.

Rick's mind flashed the most intense purple she'd ever seen and then she heard him fumbling in the drawer next to the bed.

She stilled over Thomas, just letting him rest within her, all thick and hot and hard. Her pussy muscles rippled over him and he let loose a howl nearly the equal of hers.

"I'm going to make you as much of a rogue as I am," she whispered in his ear.

Thomas grinned at her, all fangs. "It takes one to love one, Harriet love." He looked past her and noticed what Rick was up to. "Harriet, if you aren't ready for this…"

"Hush, love. I'm ready for anything."

And she was. Rick eased the tip of the lube into her rectum and shot a cool stream into her before his fingers returned, gently stretching her open. One finger, then two, then she got lost in sensation and couldn't count anymore. It felt strange, then good, then very strangely good.

Push back, Harriet love. She tried and it got easier. Then something that was definitely not his finger was easing its way past the muscular ring of her backside. Harriet stilled and waited until she felt Rick's thighs up tight against her ass cheeks.

She felt full. Full of vampire cock in front, full of psi cock behind. A werewolf sandwich, speared by her lovers.

It was amazing.

Rick leaned over her, his chest quivering with the effort he was using to just stay still. "Harriet, you feel so unbelievably fucking tight."

"Are you okay?" Thomas said quietly.

"I...I think so." As she said it, she realized that she was.

"Then let's get moving, because I'm going nuts just lying here." Thomas lifted his hips and pushed his cock up against her womb.

"Oh man. I *felt* that," Rick crowed. Harriet felt him ease back and then home again.

And I felt that!

Harriet wanted to laugh. *I felt it too.*

Slowly at first, like a carefully choreographed dance, they tried moving together, Thomas easing in and out of her pussy, Rick moving in and out of her ass, Harriet not sure which way to go, but everything she did felt simply phenomenal.

The need to climax came quickly, but before that she also felt Thomas' hunger grow. He nipped at her neck and took a little, but she knew Rick had the blood he needed the most. Rick had one arm around her waist, the other around her breasts. She helped guide Thomas' mouth to the closest wrist and felt through their link when he bit down. He fed as always, voraciously, but Harriet kept watch.

The sensation of Thomas' fangs drove Rick harder and he pumped deep into her. If she wasn't werewolf stock it might have hurt her, but as it was she barely even noticed. He paused, on the verge of orgasm, and she felt through the link that Thomas had taken as much as he could. She broke his hold on Rick's arm and drove herself down on his cock.

Behind her Rick cried out, long and hard, his cock pulsing inside her. Thomas did the same thing in front of her, his hands clenching hers. That pushed Harriet over the brink and again she howled, her cries blending with those of her two men.

Her two lovers, now and forever.

Sated, the three of them collapsed on the bed and in moments were fast asleep.

* * * * *

It was some time later that Harriet awoke, her super hearing warning of something odd. With both Rick's and Thomas' arms around her, it took a couple of minutes to disentangle herself, but when she sat up, she was sure of what she was hearing.

She poked Rick and then Thomas. "Wake up. I think we're moving."

"Moving?" Rick sat up and yawned. "Can't be. We're docked planet side."

"Perhaps we are, but I hear the engines running."

"Are you sure?" Rick looked dubious. "I can't hear them up here."

Thomas tilted his head and frowned. "But I can." He got up and headed for the comm-unit. "Elvie, why are the engines running?"

"Because we're out in space. You need to run them to get somewhere." The AI's clipped tones sounded peculiarly satisfied.

"Elvie, why are we in space?" Rick joined Thomas. "We hadn't gotten an assignment yet, and Harriet has to go to the office."

"Assignment? Office? Oh you mean those jobs of yours. Don't worry about it, I've taken care of them."

"Elvie…" Rick started to say, but Harriet interrupted him.

"What do you mean you've 'taken care of them'?"

"I mean that I submitted your resignations—all three of them—while you were sleeping." In the stunned silence, the AI made what sounded like a sigh. "Well, someone had to save you from yourselves. Rick, you and Thomas were miserable at the idea of being bounty hunters, and I can't say that I liked the idea very much either. It's just wrong for us to go hunting rogues when that's what we are ourselves."

"But Harriet…that was her dream job…"

"Was it, Harriet? You forget, I hear everything on this ship and I heard you muttering under your breath when you got home today, complaining about how tedious your job was before asking about the guys."

Harriet's cheeks heated. "The first day of any new job can be challenging—"

Elvie cut her off. "You weren't challenged…you were bored. Sitting in an office, day after day, adding up columns of numbers. That's a life sentence, not a reward."

Harriet sat down, her knees weak. It was true. She'd gotten her dream job and had been bored nearly the entire day. Adding up other people's numbers wasn't nearly as much fun as adding up her own. Running her own spreadsheets, keeping accounts…

Like keeping the accounts of a small trading operation. Just one ship.

She looked up to see the guys staring at her warily. "Harriet, if you want to go back…we can tell them it was a mistake," Thomas said. "I'm sure Bernie would understand."

"I'm sure she would too. But there are other things to consider."

"What's that?"

"Well, for one thing, Thomas, you need me to keep you from sucking Rick dry. And Rick…"

"Yes, Harriet?"

"That thing you like to do so much does not make babies. You might want to think about that."

Rick's jaw dropped. "You mean that? Harriet, honey, I'll fuck you anyway you want if you'll stay with me and Thomas."

Thomas grinned his fangy smile. "That goes for me too."

She beamed at both of them. "Then I guess it's settled. I'm staying on the *Sleepwalker* with you and Thomas. If I can't take the rogues out of you, then I guess the three of us…"

"Four!" interjected Elvie.

Harriet nodded at the comm. "Fair enough, the four of us will just have to be rogues together."

They hugged and kissed. Finally Rick said, "Of course there is still something to consider. The *Sleepwalker*'s loan is paid off so we don't have to worry about that, but there is no point in flying randomly around the galaxy. Even rogues need a way to pass the time, and a source of income."

They all sat on the bed, thinking for a moment. Thomas spoke first. "Well, there's that matter of George's client's illicit cargo. The one he mentioned back on Sedilous? That has to be delivered."

"You think he hasn't found a carrier by now?"

"We can always ask. If he has, I'm sure someone else will have a cargo to haul."

"And while we're going in that direction," Elvie added, "I just happen to have figured out where those black-market lab animals were coming from, and they're coming through a shipping station not too far from Sedilous."

"So maybe we can do some good while we're at it?" Harriet broke in. "Sounds like a plan to me."

Rick looked at Harriet and then Thomas. "Okay, Elvie, set course for Sedilous."

"Already done," she said smugly.

Epilogue
Three weeks later.

෨

A vampire, a psychic and a werewolf walk into a bar on Sedilous…they blow the whistle on a black-market operation, pick up a mysterious cargo and set off on another adventure.

The End

Enjoy an excerpt from:

I'LL BE HUNTING YOU

✷

"I miss you already. Don't leave."

Declan pressed his lips to Tori's brow and murmured, "Have to, baby."

"Then wait for me. Eli and Sarel will be here soon—tonight. Can't you wait until midnight? Dawn at the latest?"

He was tempted. When Tori got that look in her eyes it was damn near impossible to deny her. He did though. As hard as it was to deny her, ignoring the burn in his gut was even harder. Declan nuzzled her curls and whispered, "You know I can't." He shook his head. "This can't wait any longer. You have to stay here with these kids. They trust you. They feel safe with you."

Tori was silent. He pressed his lips against her temple, lingering there and savoring the warm, soft scent of her skin. "This shouldn't take too long, baby."

Then he sat up. Before he climbed out of the bed, he tucked the blankets tightly around her.

Grumbling, she closed her eyes and said, "It's already too long." Tori didn't say anything else. Rolling onto her side, she pushed up on her elbow and watched as he walked around, picking up the clothes they'd practically ripped off last night. The bite on his neck had already healed—shapeshifters healed with miraculous speed. The faint light filtering in through the blinds fell across his body, highlighting his lean, muscled form.

Her heartbeat kicked up a notch. She licked her lips and wondered if she could coax him back under the sheets for a minute. Longer. She had a bad feeling in her gut. Tori didn't want him to leave. But before she could even push her blankets down, Declan gave her a narrow look. "Don't even think about it."

Tori arched her brows and asked innocently, "What?" She could feel her fangs sliding down. Normally she could control it a little better but Declan tended to shatter her control. He always had—they'd been married for ten years. They had known each other for fifteen years.

And he *still* had this effect on her. Hunger, love and need swam through her. Rational thought became a thing of the past. Sliding out of bed, she moved toward him but before she could press her naked body against her husband's, Declan reached out and wrapped his hands around her upper arms. He eased her back and said, "Tori, come on, baby. I *have* to go."

The urgency in his voice broke through the haze of lust that fogged her brain and Tori let him usher her back to the bed. "You're no fun." A wicked grin curved her lips and she looked at him over her shoulder before crawling back under the covers. "I'll think about you when I take a shower later."

"Mean little brat," he muttered. She rolled onto her side and smiled up at him. Crouching down by the bed, Declan covered her mouth with his and kissed her smile away, his mouth rough and demanding. By the time he pulled away, they were both breathing heavily. "You do that."

He slid a palm down her side and gave her a light slap on her ass. "I have to go."

Tori watched as he finished getting dressed. Her smile faded and the lust heating her veins turned to ice. Something was wrong. She didn't know what it was but something was wrong. "Declan—"

Why an electronic book?

We live in the Information Age—an exciting time in the history of human civilization, in which technology rules supreme and continues to progress in leaps and bounds every minute of every day. For a multitude of reasons, more and more avid literary fans are opting to purchase e-books instead of paper books. The question from those not yet initiated into the world of electronic reading is simply: *Why?*

1. *Price.* An electronic title at Ellora's Cave Publishing and Cerridwen Press runs anywhere from 40% to 75% less than the cover price of the exact same title in paperback format. Why? Basic mathematics and cost. It is less expensive to publish an e-book (no paper and printing, no warehousing and shipping) than it is to publish a paperback, so the savings are passed along to the consumer.

2. *Space.* Running out of room in your house for your books? That is one worry you will never have with electronic books. For a low one-time cost, you can purchase a handheld device specifically designed for e-reading. Many e-readers have large, convenient screens for viewing. Better yet, hundreds of titles can be stored within your new library—on a single microchip. There are a variety of e-readers from different manufacturers. You can also read e-books on your PC or laptop computer. (Please note that Ellora's Cave does not endorse any specific brands. You can check our websites at www.ellorascave.com

or www.cerridwenpress.com for information we make available to new consumers.)

3. *Mobility.* Because your new e-library consists of only a microchip within a small, easily transportable e-reader, your entire cache of books can be taken with you wherever you go.

4. *Personal Viewing Preferences.* Are the words you are currently reading too small? Too large? Too... ANNOYING? Paperback books cannot be modified according to personal preferences, but e-books can.

5. *Instant Gratification.* Is it the middle of the night and all the bookstores near you are closed? Are you tired of waiting days, sometimes weeks, for bookstores to ship the novels you bought? Ellora's Cave Publishing sells instantaneous downloads twenty-four hours a day, seven days a week, every day of the year. Our webstore is never closed. Our e-book delivery system is 100% automated, meaning your order is filled as soon as you pay for it.

Those are a few of the top reasons why electronic books are replacing paperbacks for many avid readers.

As always, Ellora's Cave and Cerridwen Press welcome your questions and comments. We invite you to email us at Comments@ellorascave.com or write to us directly at Ellora's Cave Publishing Inc., 1056 Home Avenue, Akron, OH 44310-3502.

COMING TO A BOOKSTORE NEAR YOU!

ELLORA'S CAVE

Bestselling Authors Tour

Discover for yourself why readers can't get enough of the multiple award-winning publisher Ellora's Cave.

Whether you prefer e-books or paperbacks, be sure to visit EC on the web at www.ellorascave.com

for an erotic reading experience that will leave you breathless.